Alix fe of excitement

The dim light in the tent seemed to create a sense of intimacy, and a tension seemed to be building up between them.

"It's not illogical for me to want to kiss you, Alix. After all, it will be goodbye soon." Reed's voice was very soft, and as he reached for her she felt her breathing become uneven.

"Kissing my passengers goodbye is not included in the itinerary, Reed," Alix said, trying not to sound disturbed.

His hand went to her hair, sending her pulses racing. "It is now."

She tried not to respond when he kissed her. But she clung to him, wanting more. After tomorrow she would never see him again.

Wynne May was born near Johannesburg, South Africa. Shortly after graduating from college, she began working for the South African Broadcasting Corporation. While on holiday she met Claude, the handsome green-eyed stranger who spoke to her after she slipped and fell into a swimming pool! Three months later Claude slipped a diamond ring onto Wynne's finger as they stood under the stars in an exotic garden. Wynne now spends her time with her family—and writing romances.

Books by Wynne May

TOMORROW'S SUN

Wynne May

Harlequin Books

TORONTO • NEW YORK • LONDON
AMSTERDAM • PARIS • SYDNEY • HAMBURG
STOCKHOLM • ATHENS • TOKYO • MILAN

Original hardcover edition published in 1989
by Mills & Boon Limited

ISBN 0-373-17048-3

Harlequin Romance first edition 1989

The Chobe National Game Reserve does exist.
For the purpose of this novel, however,
the Grewia Safari Lodge, Sycamore Safari Lodge
and Marula Safari Lodge—and others—
exist only within these pages.

Game wardens and wildlife guides
are pure fiction.

Wynne May

CHAPTER ONE

STRAINED to screaming point, Alix Sandton shifted her position in the custom-built Land Rover so that she could look past Reed Forsythe. If Camille Boyer says one more word, I'll explode! she thought.

'Camille, please don't tell me how to run a safari, if you don't mind. I was merely pointing out that Look-Out Safaris considers it an offence to get out of a vehicle while on a game-viewing safari—unless where authorised. As your safari guide, I'm not here to bend these rules. I'm here to drive you about and to see to it that my passengers adhere to them.' She lifted her shoulders. 'You know, Botswana is twice the size of West Germany and parts of it are very wild. Chobe, for instance, is untamed and potentially dangerous. In other words, we're not in some glorified zoo. We're in a huge wildlife national park.'

'What you seem to forget, Alix, is that Africa, for me, is a huge adventure. In France, I own a gallery and I am anxious to take as many photographs as possible. Why can't you just leave me alone?' Camille's voice was raised.

'But don't you understand? There are predators out there—lions, cheetahs, leopards, hyenas...'

'Let me worry about that,' Camille retorted. 'I am responsible for my own safety. If I choose to take a chance, that is my own affair, *non*?'

Alix made no attempt, now, to calm her temper.

'I have no desire to argue with you. Just see to it that you remain inside this Land Rover. OK?'

'First it was the malaria pills,' Camille was determined to voice her complaints, 'I am informed that I must take these and I have had a constant headache—worse than the jet-lag with which I arrived. There are other aggravations.'

Alix was bristling, but when she answered, she did not raise her voice. She merely changed the tone.

'Tell me about them. It's my job to know. I'm here to handle your complaints and problems, after all, but so far as the anti-malaria pills are concerned, you don't *have* to take them. It's entirely up to you, Camille, but it's in your own interest that you do. All tourists to the reserve are advised to guard against malaria, since it's endemic in these parts. Please yourself on this issue. If you want to take a chance—well, that's all right with me. You have, in fact, signed a document to that effect.'

'I do intend to take a chance. The tablets will be disposed of as soon as I reach camp. Perhaps, since you are so cautious, Alix, you would care to avail yourself of them?'

Boldly marked Look-Out Safaris, the Land Rover was parked on the side of a corrugated, potholed track in the Chobe National Game Reserve in Botswana, and even though the elephants, like moving grey hills, had disappeared into the bush,

Alix had left the engine running to ensure a safe getaway, should the occasion present itself. The elephants had still been there, however, when Camille Boyer had opened the door and jumped from the Land Rover to take photographs.

Reed Forsythe apparently thought it time to join in the feud between the two girls. 'You're giving Alix a bad time. Come on, Camille, what is it with you?'

It was ridiculous, Alix found herself thinking, but everything about Reed attracted her, and what was more tantalising was the knowledge that he had the power to stir a disturbing reaction in her every time he accidentally touched her, which, since he always occupied the middle seat, was quite often.

In many ways, her job was frequently trying, and this particular game-viewing safari had been a difficult one. The two young French couples from the Indian Ocean island of La Réunion did not speak English, except for one or two basic phrases. Apart from a game-viewing safari, they were chiefly interested in viewing crocodiles and had visited several private crocodile farms. Camille and Reed, on the other hand, were from France, but Reed had mentioned that he had left England to study in France for two years, and had come to admire the style of the French, and he had ended up by making his home there. He also appeared to know the island, La Réunion, just as well, and he had obviously known Jacques, Jacquetta, Hugo and Mercedes for some time.

Fed up with everything, Alix turned and stared through the dust-coated windscreen. Her nerves felt jangled and she glanced at her watch. It had been another long, sundrenched day and it was, she saw, time to head back to camp. In fact, another safari was coming to an end and tomorrow would be the last day for her tourists, from France and La Réunion, who would be saying goodbye to Look-Out Safaris' luxury tents, wild game and green and gold mopane trees.

Apart from the camping grounds of the Park authorities, a number of private concerns had tented, or hutted, camps in the Chobe area, and Look-Out Safaris was one such outfit.

Two Land Rovers—both open vehicles—marked 'Look-Out Safaris' were already parked at the camp, and this indicated that Wallis Van Rijk and Sandy Douglass were already back, having spent the greater part of the day with clients, viewing wildlife. Preparing to sink from view, the sun looked like a floating crimson ball and the bush was, for this brief and magical moment, tinged with a deep rose. There were sounds of laughter coming from the direction of the Tiger Fish Bar, which overlooked the river. Apparently, guides and clients had lost no time in quenching their thirsts.

Game-viewing always seemed to end in late-afternoon visits to the tiny reed and thatch curio shop, no matter how often visitors had been there before, and Alix made a point of slowing down and stopping there, before continuing to the parking area, near the tents.

'Anyone for the curio shop?' she asked.

It appeared that everybody except Reed wanted to go, and Camille's expression was sulky as she got out of the Land Rover. Looking up at Reed, she asked, 'Why aren't you coming?'

'Because I want to soothe my nerves.' He spoke lazily.

'I am interested in a bracelet of rose-coloured agate. I would like your opinion, Reed, before I purchase it.'

'You've told me about it—the rose-coloured agate from—what was it? Bobonong? You'll buy it, anyway, whether I'm with you or not. I'll see you later. I'm longing for a drink,' said Reed, while Camille looked mutinous.

There was something undeniably stylish about Reed Forsythe, Alix was thinking as she listened to all this, although he wore clothes that were designed completely without fuss.

As she prepared to drive the short distance to the tents, she was quick to notice that he made no attempt to move over to the end seat which Camille had just vacated. Feeling his eyes on her, Alix turned and gave him a haughty honey-gold stare. 'What's wrong with your nerves, by the way?'

'My nerves?' His deep blue eyes were mocking.

'You said you wanted to soothe your nerves, a moment ago. Was it because of the feud over the elephants?'

'My friend Armand's young cousin can be a bit overpowering. I think you and I should soothe our nerves by having a drink together, Alix.'

'Do you think that would help?' Her voice was tinged with sarcasm.

The luxury tents which made up this particular camp overlooked the Chobe River, a tributary of the Zambesi, and each tent contained two beds. Like Alix, Reed and Camille were booked into separate tents, while the married couples occupied the remaining two.

Alix parked the dust-covered Land Rover and, taking the keys from the ignition, she opened the door and slid from the high seat. Her polished cotton khaki jacket was draped over the back of the seat, and as she reached for it, her eyes brooded on Reed, who was already making his way round to where she was standing. As he joined her, their eyes met, and a current seemed to pass between them. Carelessly she slipped the jacket over her shoulders while, beside her, Reed was saying, 'You have the ability to turn bush khaki into nothing short of high fashion, do you know that?'

Glancing up, she laughed lightly. 'Thank you. I didn't know, actually. The credit must go to a wonderful seamstress in Gaberone. *She* has the ability to give these trouser suits the Calvin Klein touch— though Calvin would probably be mad to hear me say that!'

'Well, I promise not to tell,' he teased.

His dark blue eyes always came as a surprise to her, she was thinking, just as the jacket which was hanging from her shoulders began to slip. With a fluid movement she caught it as it fell. As he made to help her she said quickly, 'I wasn't going to put it on, anyway. It doesn't matter.' Somehow she did not want him to touch her, and, auburn-haired, slim, tanned and utterly beautiful, she moved away from him.

As always, he was perfectly at ease in well-tailored trousers and shirt. He seemed to have everything, she thought, from health to obvious wealth. She could imagine him in car-racing gear—and of course, there would always be a beautiful woman around. Or maybe he sat behind a magnificent carved desk, upon which chrome executive toys stood offering themselves to him should he feel inclined to indulge in a few moments' relaxation during a busy day?

'By the way, I'm sorry I lost my temper back there.' Alix lifted her slim shoulders. 'I felt—really provoked.'

He laughed softly. 'As a matter of fact, Alix, I find these glimpses of your temper quite tantalising.'

'Oh?' She tried not to flap. 'Well, I mustn't keep you. You mentioned that you were longing for a drink.'

'I hate to drink alone.' The groove showed in his cheek.

'Well, I'm sure you'll sort something out, Reed.'

'I'll expect you to join me in a few minutes. I find I bought too much before we left Maun.'

She knew he was joking. 'And that's why you're inviting me for drinks—because you've bought too much for your safari, and leaving the game reserve the day after tomorrow, you want me to help you to get rid of it?' She laughed. 'Thank you!'

Flaming sunset colours of iridescent pink, shades of purple, lilac and orange were spreading over the entire sky and, caught up in this moment with Reed, Alix felt herself under his spell.

Apart from the liquor available at the small shop, the custom-built Land Rover was equipped with a deep-freeze and refrigerator, and before leaving Maun, the main gateway to the wilderness area, Reed and the French couples had seen to it that they had, between them, stocked the refrigerator with sundowner requirements to suit their own tastes.

Usually Alix linked up with other Look-Out guides who happened to be in camp; in this case Wallis Van Rijk and Sandy Douglass who, like her, wore khaki and owned bush briefcases which always seemed to be crammed with itineraries, reservation slips, scraps of information written on scraps of paper, maps, brochures and notes on petrol consumption and so on.

Actually, she thought, she was craving for a shower, but the shower could wait. The idea of being alone with Reed, while the others were at the curio shop, appealed to her.

'Fine. In a few minutes, then.' She gave him one of her slow smiles and turned away.

'Alix?'

She turned. 'Yes?'

'You have *the* most incredible eyes.'

'I do? Well, there's a thing.'

Despite their short acquaintance, she had grown to like Reed—to be excited at the sight of him. He was standing beneath the awning of his tent which was pitched on a concrete base which, as in the case of all the tents, afforded its occupant a degree of protection from damp. He had a glass of Scotch on rattling ice-cubes in his hand, and when he saw her, he put the glass down on a small camp table.

'What will you have, Alix? A shandy? Something more potent, on the other hand? You name it.' His amazing eyes went over her.

'A shandy would be perfect. Just what the doctor ordered, in fact.'

Alix felt a thrill of awareness which was crazy, she knew, for after tomorrow she would probably never see him again. The thought was depressing.

'I can't think why we haven't done this before, Alix, just the two of us. I guess you've gathered by now that the main topic of conversation around here happens to be crocodiles and crocodile farms. Sometimes it gets a bit much, believe me.'

He was, of course, referring to the conversation of the French couples who made up the party.

'What's the big interest in crocodiles? Or shouldn't I ask?' She laughed lightly.

'You shouldn't ask, but since you have, we all have a mutual friend in La Réunion. His name is Armand Leclerc and he owns a number of very attractive holiday chalets—so remember that if ever you want to go on holiday there. For some weird reason Armand has set his heart on creating a crocodile farm as a tourist attraction, among other things. The couples on safari with us are in on this project and they've come here to find out what it's all about.'

'Oh, no! How awful. I just can't imagine a crocodile farm on an island,' Alix answered.

'Well, there's already a turtle farm on the island. What Armand has in mind is what he calls a spectacular new safari world. Plans have already been drawn up, but permission not yet granted by the authorities. Anyway, there would be an underwater grotto, waterfalls, exotic reptiles, fish and even snakes. Don't shudder, Alix.'

'I can't help it! On an island!' She laughed again.

'The farm is intended as a commercial breeding centre for crocodiles. Skins will be exported to Europe and dried flesh to the Far East, I'm told, where it's a much-sought-after aphrodisiac. In addition to all this, there'd be a magnificent display of sub-tropical ferns and orchids.'

Disappointed in him, she asked, 'Where do you come in?'

'I don't. At the last minute Armand got sick and couldn't come. He was supposed to be your other passenger, by the way. He asked me to be his guest, and so I decided to join the party.'

After a moment she said, 'And Camille?'

'Armand's cousin. She was coming, anyway. She has a photographic gallery in France.'

'And so you're all very much in touch?'

'Well, I have other business involvements in La Réunion. I often go there.'

Watching him as he poured her drink, Alix went on, 'I've noticed how fluent you are in French.'

'Don't you believe it. My French is far from perfect, but I've lived in France for some time now.'

She had lowered herself into a wood and canvas chair and, after passing her the shandy, Reed sat down on the other chair and lifted his khaki-clad legs and put his feet on another camp table.

'Actually, Armand tells a story of how there was a commotion one day. A number of guests at the chalets had taken chairs and were standing on them to look at something which was on one of the lower branches of a tree. It turned out that they were excited about a chameleon, and it caused such a stir of excitement that he found himself wondering what it would be like if the chameleon had happened to be a crocodile. A chameleon, after all, has a tail and is a lizard—of sorts.'

Alix laughed outright, spluttering over her shandy.

'A crocodile, Reed, is anything but a chameleon, or a lizard. It devours people, if it gets a chance.'

He turned to look at her. When he spoke the tone of his voice was mocking. 'You may be a wildlife guide, Miss Sandton, but permit *me* to put you wise. A crocodile is indeed a thick-skinned, long-tailed amphibious tropical saurian of genus crocodilus. Saurian, permit me to advise you further, means *of* or like lizard.'

'I show people crocodiles nearly every day on a safari, but I just never thought about what you've just told me. Well, let's hope the crocodiles don't escape and terrorise the islanders and tourists.'

He asked, 'Have you known crocodiles to escape?'

Alix thought for a moment. 'No, I haven't, but that doesn't mean to say that it hasn't happened.'

'A crocodile's worst enemy is man,' he said. 'I know that. I'm perfectly aware that he has no intention of ending up as a handbag or a pair of shoes. In many regions crocodile meat is considered a delicacy. I guess he knows that too.'

'There's an old African proverb which says, he who feeds the crocodile gets eaten last. Armand had better just watch out, Reed.'

'Let's put it another way, Alix. When I begin to question the idea of Armand's farm, I'm sharply reminded that if it were not for crocodile farms, there would probably be few crocodiles left in the world. After all, they're also bred to supply zoos and to restock areas where they occur naturally.'

'An island isn't "naturally",' she answered. 'I'm afraid, to me, breeding crocodiles on an island is a crazy idea. Your friend Armand Leclerc needs his head read!'

Reed laughed at that. 'For sure.'

'And here we are, talking crocodiles again, and I'm to blame,' she laughed. 'You'll be sorry you offered me a drink in a moment, won't you?'

'I won't be sorry. I'm only sorry it hasn't happened before.' He took a long breath. 'You know, Alix, this peace will be all I ever think about when I get back...for a while, anyway.'

For a while... Alix glanced at his hand, which held the glass, and in the lamplit semi-darkness she noticed that it was strong and tanned, the fingers well shaped.

'It's not all peace. What about the hippos last night? They made enough noise. It was incredible!'

Reed was saying, 'I always seem to hear countless other animal noises and puzzling, rustling movements which make my hair stand on end.'

'Oh, come!' Her slow smile, as always, was beautiful—and slightly mocking. 'You surprise me. Don't you just love the fiendish laughter of a hyena? I do.'

'I bet you do.' They both laughed and she did not enlighten him that, with all her safari experience, she always felt the same way, especially when the accommodation happened to be in tents.

There was a small silence, and Reed broke it.

'How is it, Alix, that a girl like you chooses to chase the sun in search of wild animals?'

She finished her shandy and put the glass on the small table beside her. 'Oh, chasing the sun has its compensations, believe me. For one thing, there's that wonderful peace you were talking about a little while ago.'

He got up and came round to the table and reached down for her empty glass. 'Despite the Calvin Klein touch to your khaki trouser suits, you strike me as a career girl,' he said.

A moment later she was raising her slim, sun-bronzed hand and taking a sip of the shandy which he had just poured for her. A wave of annoyance swept over her.

'And you don't think this,' she made a gesture with her hand, 'is a career. Is that it?'

'Ah, tuck your claws in, Alix! I didn't exactly say that.'

'No, not exactly. But you implied it.'

'Come on!' he laughed softly.

'This is my career. I changed my life-style, which used to be advertising—in Zimbabwe. It was exciting. My folks are there. My father is a tobacco farmer, but with all the anti-smoking slogans around I'm reluctant to mention it. Then I met Karl Sievewright. Karl was on holiday in Zimbabwe and he offered me a job with Look-Out Safaris. At first I worked in the office in Maun, which is the base of a number of recognised safari operators—Look-Out, to name but one. Then I did a wildlife course and became the owner of a guide licence. I'm also a member of the Kalahari Conservation Society. The pace of my working day, Reed, hasn't changed all that much, believe me. It's still hectic and it certainly doesn't lack the adrenalin to keep me alive. I realise, of course, that I won't want to be doing this in another, say,' she lifted her shoulders, 'three to four years' time.'

'Don't press your luck, Alix,' he cautioned.

'What do you mean by that?'

'You might get chased by a rogue elephant one day.'

'How do you know it hasn't already happened?' she laughed. 'I've been chased before today, make no mistake.' There was a small silence and then she went on, 'Guides are not supposed to be pushy, but I've been wondering about you, as it so happens.'

Reed got up to pour himself another drink and she watched him as he splashed Scotch on to ice cubes which lay at the bottom of the glass. He glanced up. 'I'm curious, Alix.'

'You hardly appear to be the type who would be content to have a guide drive you around,' she explained. 'I should have thought you would have preferred to hire one of our Land Rovers and drive it yourself. You could have stayed at the famous Chobe Safari Lodge. In fact, there are a number of small lodges, chalets and hotels throughout the north-east. Look-Out owns one which is quite unabashedly luxurious.'

'Maybe I'll come back and do that,' he told her. 'Don't forget, I didn't book this safari. Armand was responsible for the arrangements. In any case, being driven around suited me. I'd been burning the candle at both ends, actually, and I felt like a good rest.'

Feeling ridiculously jealous, Alix said, 'You sound quite a—playboy.'

He laughed. 'Is that how I appear to you? Well, well! I just never seem to know when to call a day a day. I'm perpetually rushing to catch early morning flights to other parts of France and even to other countries. And then I rush to catch flights home. There are, among other things, long and late meetings to put up with—and there you have it.'

After a moment she asked, 'What is your occupation? Or shouldn't I ask?'

'It's no secret. I have a number of business ventures going, but about an hour's train journey from Paris—north of Paris—there's Chantilly. You've heard of it, I'm sure. Most of Chantilly's inhabitants are involved in a thriving racehorse industry. I have a stud farm there.'

'Really? It sounds exciting.' Alix was wondering about the woman or women in his life.

At that moment Camille arrived on the scene, and it was easy to see the anger that flared across her beautiful face when she saw Alix sitting in the lamplight with Reed.

'I've been looking for you,' she said to Reed. 'I thought we were going to have a drink together?'

'What would you like?' He stood up.

'The usual—what else?' she replied. 'You know what I like by now.'

'What about the bracelet?' he asked easily. 'Did you buy it?'

'Yes—and without your help. Also, I got two large tribal masks for my gallery. They will be sent direct to France.' Camille's gaze in Alix's direction was nothing short of hostile.

Alix stood up. 'Thank you for the drink,' she said to Reed. 'I've enjoyed being with you and having a chat.'

'We'll see you later, Alix.'

'Fine.'

He came to watch her as she walked in the direction of her own tent. In her tent, Alix looked out a fresh chintz-khaki trouser suit and, gathering her things together, she went to the ablution building, since that was the pattern of things in a tented camp. She revelled in a cascade of warm water and then dried herself and rubbed oil of geranium on her legs and arms.

When she was dressed she put on her antique Ethiopian bracelet of exotic amber and gold beads and then fastened the matching necklace around her neck. Both items had cost her a fortune. Her strappy sandals were the colour of cinnamon and had medium-height heels. Even in the wilderness, it was common practice among tourists to appear a little outrageous at night—and why should this not also apply to a guide? she reasoned. She was perfectly aware, however, that these touches of glamour on her part—as the only female guide working for Look-Out Safaris—irked Wallis Van Rijk. Tanned, silver-haired and sarcastic-looking, Wallis had made it perfectly clear from the beginning that he strongly objected to Look-Out Safaris' decision to employ Alix. Maybe...she smiled at the thought...she added these touches of audacity to her safari outfits just to anger Wallis? Well, too bad for him. She disliked him as much as he obviously disliked her.

The repetitive beats of a tom-tom told her it was time to leave for dinner.

Catering for fourteen guests, three guides and the necessary camp staff, the cane-furnished lounge, dining area and a second pub were constructed from cement blocks, painted white. A soaring thatched roof, intermingled with dark beams and poles, completed the very Out-of-Africa scene. The pub, which was merely a long cement affair, painted white and topped with shining wood, was at the far end. The stools were cane, as were the low tables and chairs arranged between the pub and the dining area, where four tables had been placed on either side of the room to form two long tables. The tablecloths and napkins were made of crimson linen and there was no shortage of lamps, which cast a rich glow over everything.

Unlike the tiny and flimsily constructed curio shop, reception area and Tiger Fish Bar, this building was solid. It was just a matter of preference when it came to pubs, but sunset seemed to be the popular time for the Tiger Fish pub, which was made of reeds and thatch and which was high enough off the ground to be secure and yet close enough to hear and see the hippos. At night, one of the big thrills was to hear a lion roaring its challenge to the stars. Before dinner, most people seemed to prefer meeting up in the dining area, however.

By the time Alix arrived her tourists from France and the island of La Réunion—with the exception of Reed Forsythe—were already seated on cane stools at the bar. So were the guests who were being guided by Wallis and Sandy.

Alix took the seat near to Sandy Douglass, and then she noticed Reed coming towards them. As usual, he generated a certain spark of electricity that turned female heads. Alix pretended not to be aware of him, as he went to sit next to Camille. He had no right to be so devastatingly handsome, she found herself thinking, as he bent his head to Camille, who had whispered something to him. Once Alix looked up from her glass to find him staring at her and, feeling caught out, she smiled briefly and glanced away.

Everybody in the small camp, if one happened to listen in, was discussing the events of the day, which of course revolved around game-spotting, photography and 'narrow squeaks'. Wallis and Sandy amused the guests with a number of hair-raising stories.

Later, Alix sat with Wallis and Sandy at dinner, which was served by three waiters of the Tawana tribe wearing long white trousers, tunics and turbans. When the meal was over she went back to her tent and took her briefcase to the outdoor area beneath the awning where, by glowing lamplight, she began to sort through papers concerning the safari. There were lamps on the tables on the outdoor areas of all the tents, and from where she was sitting she could see Jacques, Jacquetta, Mercedes and Hugo, from La Réunion, talking with an animation usual in them.

Camille was sitting outside her tent with Reed, and Alix felt a stab of irritation when she thought about the way in which she'd had to keep checking the girl for getting in and out of the Land Rover whenever she felt like it. Thinking about every-thing now, Alix realised that she would be more than thankful to see the back of Camille, but saying goodbye to Reed Forsythe was going to be another matter—not that she had got to know him all that well, but she realised that she would have liked to. This was one of the not-so-good aspects of her job—this having to say goodbye to people she'd grown to like and whom she would never see again.

She went to bed, and although she read by lamplight until her eyes were drooping she had difficulty in falling asleep. She lay listening to the animal noises and feeling some tension, just as she always did when the accommodation happened to be in tents. She also thought about Gerald Phipps, in Gaberone, and about Reed Forsythe, who attracted her more than any man she had ever known. She was depressed at the thought of having to say goodbye to him.

More game-viewing followed in the morning, and they left the camp as the sun was beginning to daub the white walls of the ablutions block and the main building with dark pink. Even the tents seemed to take on a flushed tint.

After lunch, which had been prepared and packed for them by the cook and which they had at an authorised camping site, Camille was full of her usual complaints.

'I am so frustrated! I have not been able to get one good shot of lions. If only I could get out of the Land Rover! Next time I return to Africa...' Oh, God forbid! groaned Alix to herself, '...I will book for a game trackers' camp, where I can leave the camp on my own two feet and walk with the game rangers and the trackers.'

Listening to her, Alix struggled to keep her temper under control, and decided to keep her mouth shut.

The landscape continued to slide by and each bush claimed the attention of everybody, for the simple reason that it might be hiding a pride of lions, or even an elusive leopard.

In the afternoon, when they least expected it, they came upon four panting, tawny big cats. They lay, suffering from heat, beneath a camel-thorn tree, and the Land Rover was no sooner at a standstill than Camille opened the door on her side and slid down from the seat. Almost immediately her Nikon went into operation, the metallic whirring plainly heard and immediately creating tension.

For a moment Alix's heart seemed to stop with shock, and then she gasped, 'Oh, God! Can you believe this?' In the back of the Land Rover Jacquetta and Mercedes began shrieking hysterically, while their husbands shouted at them to keep calm.

'I'll handle her,' said Reed, and before Alix could stop him, he was out of the vehicle.

'Move over,' he ordered furiously, a moment later, 'next to Alix. What the devil do you think you were doing?'

Camille swung round on him. 'How dare you push me around like this? I would have survived very well without you!'

Alix cut in. 'Do you know, Camille, I've conducted more safaris than I can remember, but *you* are the most difficult person I've ever had in my Land Rover.'

'Really, Alix? Well, that is too bad, *non*? What is all the fuss about? Personally, I do not believe the lion deserves the title of king of the beasts. Look, they have not even moved. They are quite docile and, so far as I am concerned, incredibly foolish.'

The animals had, in fact, shown little concern— except for a growing interest which revealed itself in green eyes and an occasional flicker of tails.

'I give up!' Alix's voice contained all the anger she was feeling. 'Just what are you trying to suggest, Camille? That lions, contrary to common belief, *fundamentally* are really very friendly animals and not at all wild or aggressive? Well, allow me to put you wise. You were just lucky that there were no cubs about.'

Camille laughed at that. 'Oh, come! Your imagination runs away with you.'

'Weren't you aware that your life was in danger?' Reed asked angrily.

'No. I was completely unaware of it, because it was not.'

'What kind of dumb remark is that?' Reed went on. 'Those are not domestic cats out there. This could have ended in disaster.'

'But it did not.' Camille drew the words out sarcastically. 'Unlike you, I am not going to waste time speculating about whether I would have been devoured or not.'

Alix thought she would explode with frustrated rage, and she took it out on Reed.

'Reed, if your girlfriend had wanted this sort of excitement why *didn't* you arrange for a game trackers' safari? *My* job is tailored to drive my party around in a *closed* Land Rover and to act as their guide. Everybody I drive around is supposed to stay inside the vehicle, except at authorised camping grounds and picnic spots. I've explained this over and over again. Right?'

'What about the open Land Rover which is behind us right at this moment?' Camille asked, while Alix's eyes went to the rear-view mirror and her heart skipped a beat when she saw Wallis Van Rijk and party parked behind them. Had the open Land Rover been there when Camille and Reed were out of the Land Rover?

Camille was determined to go on causing unpleasantness. 'How is it that we are never permitted to go out in these open Land Rovers—only the same people, day after day? Why, in other words, have we been allotted a closed vehicle?'

'Ask Reed,' snapped Alix. 'His friend—your cousin, when it comes to that—arranged this with Look-Out Safaris.'

By this time Reed had had enough. 'You're going on like an enraged cat, Alix. Pipe down!'

Her honey-gold eyes were glittering. 'Just who do you think you're talking to? You amaze me! You take this girl's part...'

'I do *not* take her part...'

'I'm not just off the boat, Mr Forsythe!'

'And don't you be too sure about that, Miss Sandton,' he answered angrily. 'And now, have you both finished?'

'Quite finished.' Alix started the engine.

As she drove back to camp, Alix tried to console herself that her difficulties with Camille Boyer were nearly over.

She was sitting outside her tent after dinner, when Reed invited himself over, and the sight of him evoked an angry, if excited, response in her. Her moody eyes followed his movements as he sat down near her and stretched out his legs.

'You're still very upset, I think, Alix. You didn't turn up at the pub and you only came to dinner when everyone was just about ready to leave.'

'I was late for the simple reason that I had things to do. Anyway, Reed, I've learned not to *stay* upset.'

Since she did not want him to go back to France with conflicting thoughts about the game-viewing safari she said, 'It's easy to become over-excited and carried away in a situation like we were in today. Forget it.'

'Oh, I can accept that it's easy to become over-excited, Alix, but Camille forgets to toe the line more often than not. Apart from that, it's been a most enjoyable safari and I'd like to thank you personally for being so patient with us.'

'I'm afraid I wasn't all that patient—but thank you, anyway.'

'I'll think of nothing else, after I get home,' Reed went on. 'The peace at the end of each day; the

incredible feeling of lying between freshly laun-
dered and sun-dried sheets at night and listening to
the sounds of wild animals. It's going to be hard
to adjust for a while,' he said.

Join the club, Alix was thinking. What am I going
to do without *you* around?

'And what about you, Alix?'

She thought for a moment. 'Well, I'll have a few
days at home and then I'll be back here again, in
the Chobe.'

'Where is home?'

'I have a relationship going with a cottage in
Gaberone. It's always there, waiting.'

'And you enjoy living in Gaberone?' he asked.

'Yes, I do. I'm very happy there—I have some
good friends. I'll be there for some time to come—
I should imagine so, anyway. I'll probably feel the
urge to move on one day. Who knows?'

'And that's the only love-affair? With a cottage?
I can't believe that, Alix.'

'There is somebody, of course. Nothing terribly
serious.' Her thoughts flew to Gerald.

'Does he . . . ?'

'No, he doesn't!' she cut in, anticipating Reed's
question. 'He lives in a penthouse in Gaberone.
Actually, when I come to think of it, I have some
photos of the cottage, before and after. I renovated
it—you know the sort of thing. Would you like to
see them?'

'I would, yes,' he answered.

'I'll get them. They're in my bag.' She stood up,
and he joined her.

'May I come in?'

Her response was cautious. 'Well, if you like.'

As she walked ahead of him he was saying, 'This is just like going into my own tent.'

'Well, a tent is a tent, after all. What did you expect? Something out of the Arabian Nights?' Alix was feeling ruffled.

While she was getting the photos and to make conversation she said, 'You'd like our private camp. It's a *hutted* camp and is only hired as a complete unit—for a family, or a party of close friends.' The attraction she felt for him was making her feel uneasy.

As Reed took the coloured prints from her, their fingers touched and she felt a thrill of excitement.

'I can see where the love-affair comes in,' he said.

'It's cute, isn't it?' she agreed.

He gave the photos back to her. The dim light seemed to create a sense of intimacy and a tension seemed to be building up between them. Alix noticed the brooding, penetrating expression in his dark blue eyes.

'It's not illogical for me to want to kiss you, Alix. After all, it will be goodbye soon.' His voice was very soft, and as he reached for her hand, she immediately felt her breath becoming uneven. He began to stroke her wrist with his thumb and then he moved closer so that they were almost touching.

As his arms closed about her she said, 'Kissing my passengers goodbye is not included in the itinerary, Reed.'

His hand went to her hair, sending her pulse racing.

'It's on your itinerary now, Alix.'

She tried not to respond when he kissed her. He smelled of Givenchy aftershave. As he kissed her and tantalised her by lifting the pressure of his lips before pressing down again she clung to him, wanting more. He drew away from her to say, 'God, you're lovely, Alix! Do you realise what you're doing to my blood pressure right now?'

She experienced real, shattering shock, for after tomorrow she would never see him again—unless he came up with something.

'I'm going to miss you and I'll think of you constantly,' he told her.

Trying to hate him, she said, 'Well, that's a great consolation. I'd *like* that.' What was so great about him, anyway? she asked herself, trying to soothe her ruffled feelings.

At that moment Camille called out, 'Reed? Are you there?' There was petulance in her voice. 'You said . . .'

'I *know* what I said. I'll be with you in a few minutes.' He was frankly irritable.

Feeling abandoned and marooned, Alix drew away from him, resenting the other girl's claim on him.

'I'm expecting Sandy Douglass at any minute,' she lied.

'I see. In that case, goodnight, Alix. Sleep well.'

'Oh, you can count on that,' she laughed lightly, and turned away from him. 'Goodnight.'

What part did Camille Boyer play in his life? she wondered, and then decided she didn't want to know.

CHAPTER TWO

LOOKING stunning in a soft khaki trouser suit and an olive-green satin blouse, Alix was being thanked in French mingled with a smattering of English for a most enjoyable safari.

Her honey-gold eyes went to the young couples who had been her passengers for two weeks.

'Enjoy your visit to the Victoria Falls and the private crocodile farm you're going to. Have fun, Mercedes. You too, Jacquetta, Hugo, Jacques...it's been wonderful having you. I'll think of you all, *often*.'

Suddenly everybody in the courtesy bus parking area in front of Look-Out Safaris in Gaberone, where the safari had ended, seemed to be reaching for their luggage, and Alix found herself alone with Reed Forsythe.

As casually as she could she said, 'Reed...well, it's been nice having you. Have fun in Zimbabwe.'

Transport was waiting to take the party to the Holiday Inn, and Reed glanced around impatiently. 'Well, *au revoir*, Alix. I'll be in touch.'

'Sure—maybe in another world. Right?'

'I wouldn't put it like that.' Their eyes met.

'No? How would you put it?' As a defence against the depression she was feeling her voice was flippant. The memory of his handsome face and dark blue eyes was going to tantalise her for a long time.

'I'll think of something,' he said.

'I'm sure you're an expert. Anyway, good luck.' As she turned away she thought, I'll never see him again. I can't believe it. It's not fair!

How she envied him! Once the rest of his tour was over and he was on that plane and the stewardess had brought him his first drink, Alix Sandton would be forgotten. Nothing like this had happened to her before on a safari, and she was going to take good care it didn't happen again.

She made her way to the office, where she completed all the paperwork which went towards winding up the safari, then she picked up her car and was soon easing it into the messy late-afternoon Gaberone traffic.

The rose bushes which grew in fat terracotta pots had decided to welcome her home with a show of fantastic pink blooms—the kind of blooms ladies used to wear on the wide brims of their hats, years ago. Thank goodness her part-time gardener had remembered to keep them watered, she thought.

She had arranged for the cottage to be painted a dusky pink, and a half-moon cinnamon and white sun-awning framed the carved door, which had cost her a fortune. In her present depressed mood she thought what an extravagance that door was.

Like a colicky baby who had just heard its mother's footsteps, the phone started screaming to be picked up the moment Alix opened the door and, dropping her bag and holdall on to the white-tiled

floor of the small entrance hall, she made a dash
to answer it.

'Hello? Alix Sandton.'

'So you're back from that desolate scrubland?'
Gerald's voice was sarcastic and this annoyed her
immediately.

'Yes—but look, I'm busy right now. . . .'

'What doing?' he asked.

'Getting into the cottage. I've just got in—I
opened the door as the phone started ringing. I'm
dropping with fatigue, Gerald. I'll ring you back.
OK?' She dragged restless fingers through her hair.

'No, it's not OK.' She could imagine his hand-
somely thin face. His ice-blue eyes would be narrowed. He seemed to think he owned her, and the
fact that she would not go to bed with him was a
constant thorn in his side—that, and her work as
a safari guide.

'Why don't you give up this crazy job? If you
did, maybe you wouldn't always be dropping with
fatigue the moment you get back. But there it
is . . . some time next week you'll be on your way
again. What do you get out of that?' he asked.

'If that's all you phoned me about, I'll ring off.'
Alix's eyes were angry. 'Gerald, you've caught me
at a bad time. In fact, my luggage is still at my feet
where I dropped it the moment I heard the phone.
What I want right at this moment is to open all the
windows and let some fresh air into the cottage.
After all those showers in the Chobe, I'm craving
for a bath, actually.'

'I'll book a table at the Baobab,' Gerald told her, 'and I'll pick you up at seven.' There was a pause. 'Right?'

'No, it's not right. Make it seven-thirty. I'll only be ready then, and—Gerald?'

'Yes?'

'Don't be so presumptuous. After all, you don't own me.' She put the receiver down.

A few moments later she had stripped and wrapped herself in a towel, then she turned on the taps. The water cascaded into the apricot marble bath—another extravagance on her part. She added bubble bath and scented oils, and began to forget about the extravagances and to feel pampered, which was what her cottage and her life-style was all about.

The foam of bubbled and perfumed water awaited her pleasure, and she was soon stretched out in it and, closing her eyes, she began to think about the safari, and the safari, of course, meant Reed Forsythe. As the memory of his tanned face, deep blue eyes and dark hair taunted her, she was aware of a terrible sense of loss.

She also thought about Gerald, debating with herself as to whether she was—or, in fact, ever *had been*—in love with him, or whether she had just drifted into a situation where she found herself being monopolised by him. This state of affairs, she realised, had been partly created by her work as a guide, where she had to go away a lot, and then, by the time she got back, it seemed easier just to spend her leisure times with him.

Right now, the last thing she felt like doing was going out with him, but after a few minutes she stood up in the bath, soap bubbles still clinging to her long tanned body.

Since the Baobab had just recently opened its elegant doors, she decided to wear the black slipper-satin suit and the white frothy organdie blouse.

They argued incessantly during dinner, and Alix began to wonder what she had ever seen in Gerald, who was wearing his habitual expression of cynicism. Suddenly she found him extremely irritating. He was, she mused, staring at him, a carbon copy of a number of young reps. He lived in a young-executive apartment—which he referred to as his penthouse—in a new building. The rent was more than he could afford. He never stopped referring to the fact that he'd done a Dale Carnegie course. Fair-skinned, fair-haired and blue-eyed, he was always immaculately dressed. He drove a company car and carried an intricately designed briefcase. How he ever managed to open it without the help of a computer was a mystery.

He wanted to make love to her. Now, as he picked up his wine glass and settled back in his chair, he said, 'You must think I'm made of stone! We're supposed to have a relationship going, but not seriously enough for you to let me near you.'

'We might have a relationship going, as you refer to it, but I don't think I've ever given you cause to believe I'm ready for a heavy relationship, Gerald,' she retorted.

'Apart from anything,' he went on, 'you're like a child, with that doll's house of yours. Apart from your job, you think of nothing else!' His temper was rising. 'And talking about our relationship, what do you want me to do—beg for it?'

Alix felt fury flooding right through her. 'Perhaps we'd better end it right now?' She went on staring at him. 'May your next relationship be a long and *active* one!'

'While you save all your energies for game-viewing, is that it? I often wonder what the big attraction is there, anyway. There must be times, I should imagine, when you meet some guy who really tempts you.'

'Sometimes you can be so vile, Gerald. Half the time I don't know what's going on in your mind.'

'Half the time you're never here,' he snapped.

'I don't get this.' Alix took an unsettled breath. 'You must know I have no long-range plans about you. For that matter, short of getting me into bed with you, you have no long-range plans about me— so what are we going on about?'

'Look, let's enjoy ourselves,' he said. 'I don't want to fight with you, Alix.'

'I don't want to fight with you either, but...'

'What do you think of this place?' he asked.

She glanced around. 'Well, it's exciting. It's about time some of the other places were made to sit up and take notice. I like it.'

Later, Gerald said, 'I've got to go to Swaziland for a while. I'll ring you when I get back. Think of me, Alix.'

She spent the next few days attending to banking affairs, shopping, having her hair styled in the sleek way she liked it and generally enjoying the cottage. She enjoyed sleeping in her luxurious big bed with its comfortable mattress, cool sheets and lace-covered pillows. She had gone to a lot of trouble arranging for the satin bedcover to be quilted, and the rather long wait had been worth it. She had fallen in love with the expensive Impressionistic floral fabric in blue, pink, green and deep coral, and after throwing caution to the winds, she had finally bought it to cover the two plump sofas and chairs in the lounge. Her mother had sent her the cut-down country-style table which served as a coffee table between the sofas.

By knocking out one wall, a miserably dark porch had been included in the kitchen area, and here again, Alix had invested in everything from a marble pastry slab to a compact butcher's block. Wonderfully real-looking silk plants—because she was away so much and could not take care of growing plants—cascaded from baskets suspended from a massive bluegum beam stretched across the kitchen—and very essential, as it happened, since the porch wall had been knocked out to enlarge the entire area.

This, thought Alix, as she took time off to relax in her white hammock, which she'd brought back from Portugal, was what *her* life was all about for as long as she chose to live in Botswana. She had spent a lot of time, energy and money creating her home.

And then, grabbing her safari bags together, she was off to what Gerald called the desolate scrubland again. This time her passengers were from Germany, and throughout the tour she thought more about Reed Forsythe than she did of Gerald Phipps. Her honey-gold eyes were often moody, as memories came flooding in.

When she got back to Gaberone, it was to discover that she was in trouble.

Getting up to greet her and coming round from his desk, Karl Sievewright said, 'What the hell are you trying to do to Look-Out Safaris, Alix?'

Puzzled, she asked, 'What do you mean? I don't understand what this is about.'

'You don't?' His sarcastic tone angered her.

'No, I don't. Are you getting at me about something?'

He sighed loudly. 'Sit down. Let me refresh your memory.' He went back to his chair. 'Perhaps you can explain this lot?'

Alix watched him as he reached for an envelope and shook two postcard-size coloured prints from it. He almost threw the photos across the desk.

The photos were of Camille Boyer standing outside the Land Rover, her Nikon camera raised to her eye, as she photographed four lions, and of Reed, next to her. Looking at them, Alix felt slightly disorientated. A little wildly, she was thinking of the open Land Rover which had stopped behind them. Her nerves tightened. Wallis Van Rijk!

Karl swivelled his chair round and stared out of the window for a moment, before he swung back to look at her.

'Where did you get these?' asked Alix.

'What does it matter where I got them from, Alix? But in any case, Wallis Van Rijk took them.'

'The sneaky little rat!' she exclaimed furiously.

'Oh, I don't agree, Alix. This sort of irresponsible behaviour on the part of tourists and guides has to be stamped out. We've just been advised about a forthcoming article which will be appearing in a wildlife magazine shortly. In fact, these same bloody pictures—if Wallis has anything to do with it—might well feature in the magazine, with Look-Out Safaris standing out in bold letters for everyone to see. For God's sake, Alix, what were you thinking about, huh?'

'Karl, you're not going to believe this, but...'

'You're damn right I'm not going to believe it, Alix! There's the evidence, right? Within springing distance of those beasts this fool of a girl calmly whirrs away with her camera. In the next picture—*two*, not one—*two* of your passengers are out of the Land Rover now, while you're calmly sitting watching them.'

'That's just not true! You don't even know what was going on inside that Land Rover. Besides, you asked me to explain, Karl. Why don't you give me a chance?' Alix's eyes were beginning to glitter as she tried to control her anger.

Karl sat back in his chair and shrugged his shoulders.

'OK, go ahead, Alix, I'm all ears.'

'Thank you.' Her voice was crisp with burning fury. 'I had trouble with this girl right from the start. She was impossible! Do you think this,' she glanced at the coloured prints, 'had my blessing? You must be joking! Nevertheless, I still think it was a sneaky thing for Wallis Van Rijk to have done.'

'Sneaky?' Karl spoke with an obvious show of impatience. 'I don't know about sneaky. He was just doing what he knows to be right. As he pointed out, tourists are showing less and less concern towards regulations which exist, permit me to remind you, for their own safety, but when guides start permitting this, the situation becomes out of hand. Perhaps this sort of thing, with you, has been going on for some time? This would explain Wallis trailing you, maybe.'

'It hasn't been going on, I tell you! Wallis happened to be in the same area for the simple reason that we were both heading back to camp at the end of the day. The lions were very near to the camp, as a matter of fact. I like most people, but . . .'

'But you don't like Wallis, is that it? Well, Alix you're going to like him even less now, because I'm going to suspend you for a while. You'll spend the next three weeks or so in our Maun office. It just depends on my mood for how long.'

Feeling absolutely stunned, Alix recovered sufficiently to show some of her fiery spirit.

'I'm not a school kid, Karl. I'm not going to do it, and that's that.' She drew a sharp breath. 'I'll see Wallis Van Rijk in hell first!'

Karl sat back and peaked his fingertips. 'So? What do you intend to do, Alix? What do you suggest, eh?' His eyes were nasty, and it was the first time she had known him to be like this, but, thinking suddenly of what she still owed on the cottage—the marble bath and vanity basin alone, plus various other items—she said, 'That girl was back in the Land Rover in a matter of seconds. Reed Forsythe, her—well, I don't quite know what the set-up is there, but...'

'Spare me the family tree, Alix. I'm not interested.'

This remark earned Karl a furious look. 'I want to explain. Contrary to how it looks in the photos, he had got *out* to get her *in*.'

'OK, but if you'd had your wits about you, this would never have happened in the first place. Anyway, you'll do a stint in the Maun office—like it or lump it. It's up to you. It might make you think next time.'

'But why Maun?' Alix's thoughts were revolving around the small and remote frontier town which was a place of Land Rovers, Calcrete, sand and flood plains. It was a tourist jump-off point. Until recent times, she thought bitterly, Maun was so rugged that four-wheel vehicles were needed to navigate its main street.

'Because you've already worked there. You know the ropes.' Karl began to flick through the covers of several folders which were scattered about his desk. He knocked over a wooden carving of a giraffe and cursed, and Alix felt her blood beginning to boil. She felt so angry and so frustrated she could have broken down and wept loudly. 'Why not here? In Gaberone?'

'Because, my dear girl, you happen to be needed in Maun, not here. Now make up your mind.' Karl picked up his phone and began dialling.

Alix realised that the interview, so far as he was concerned, was over—take it or leave it. She knew, with a bitter heart, that she would have to take it, until she could sort something else out, for she was damned if she was going to stay on at Look-Out Safaris.

For three and a half frustrating weeks she worked in the frontier town, having, as was the policy, flown there from Gaberone, after leaving her car in the staff parking area at the back of the Look-Out offices. She had booked into the hotel and tried to make the best of things in this starting or finishing point of all Land Rover safaris. She had her small tape deck and enough *Cosmopolitan* magazines to see her through the lonely evenings. Gamely she made out requisitions, organised equipment and supplies, hired out Land Rovers to those tourists wishing to arrange specialised safaris, tailored to their own needs.

Situated on the banks of the Thamalakane River, the town was served by shops and garages. It was sun-drenched, but it was also blessed with shade because of the tall riverine forest and surrounding proclaimed wildlife sanctuary. It always amazed Alix that there was this river in an otherwise arid setting. Waterlilies adorned the river, which was home to numerous fish, aquatic birds and crocodiles, which made her think about the French couples from the island of La Réunion, and thinking about them made her brood on Reed Forsythe.

In her free time she amused herself by visiting the curios and handicraft sellers, and, squeamish as she was, she even joined a party of Americans who wanted to buy game skins and who wanted to acquaint themselves with the tanners who specialised in this.

Just when she felt like giving up, she had a phone call from Karl requesting her to catch a plane back to Gaberone.

'I've been thinking of walking out,' she told him. 'I'm surprised you even remembered....'

'Get over here, Alix, and not so much old buck,' he cut in. 'I have the details of your next safari waiting for you. Are you listening to me?'

'Yes, Karl.' The tone of her voice was sarcastic.

'I'll see you, then. Give my regards to Maun.' He rang off, and, with the receiver still in her hand, Alix began to laugh with the pleasure she was feeling.

She was looking glamorous in pricey designer jeans and a strappy white lawn camisole when she walked into the reception office in Gaberone. Karl, she was told by Maggie, was expecting her, so Alix went straight through to his office.

At first she did not recognise him. Reed Forsythe had grown a beard and a moustache. He was even more tanned and he looked terrific.

'Reed! What on earth are you doing back here?' She laughed a little breathlessly.

'One safari with Alix Sandton as guide wasn't enough, so I decided to talk the others into being my guests on another, before going back to La Réunion. By the others I'm referring to Hugo and Mercedes. Jacques and Jacquetta had to leave as planned, and...'

Alix was so thrilled that she cut in, 'And so—you haven't—I mean, you've come straight back from Zimbabwe and organised another safari?'

He gave her one of his devastating smiles. 'How are you, Alix?'

'Great.' She laughed a little and shoved her fingers through her sleek auburn hair.

'Reed has come in to discuss a change in the itinerary he'd planned with me, Alix. His guests have decided to do their own thing first, before joining up with the safari. They're going to charter a plane to Francistown. They've got to hear about the Museum and Art Gallery and they're interested to view the collection of mounted wild animals of Botswana.'

In the mood to agree with anything at the moment, Alix said, 'Oh, I'm sure they won't be disappointed. The painted dioramas are masterpieces on their own.'

Karl passed her a folder. 'Taking it from there, Alix—you're to fly to Maun with Reed, since he doesn't want to go to Francistown. You'll stock up with supplies and so on before the others arrive a few hours later. Since you'll be leaving Maun later than you usually do on a safari, you'll spend the first night at the Grewia Lodge which, as you are aware, is this side of the Moremi gates.'

After discussing the itinerary for a while longer Alix got up to leave, and so did Reed. He walked with her to where her car was parked outside the office.

In her most casual voice she said, 'Where *are* the others, by the way? Hugo and Mercedes?'

'They're lounging about the Holiday Inn. I've hired a car, for the day. Perhaps we could have lunch together, Alix?'

'I like the beard. It suits you,' she said.

'I was determined not to waste time shaving on *this* safari,' he told her.

'The others must have been keen to do this all over again. Of course, it will be a different safari. No tents, this time, I see. I'm sure you'll enjoy it.'

'I'll bring some rope along in case we have to tie Camille to the seat,' Reed said carelessly, and his remark caused a surge of disappointment, followed by fury, to pass right through her. Camille! Not again!

After a moment she said, 'So Camille has also chosen to stay on in Botswana?'

'I'm afraid so. I promised Armand I'd look after her, as it so happens,' Reed explained. 'I didn't know what I was in for, to be quite honest.'

'It's nothing to joke about! Camille just about got me dismissed from Look-Out Safaris, by the way.'

He looked at her in surprise. 'I don't understand, Alix. Why was that?'

'Can't you guess?'

'No, of course not.'

'Well, she was photographed by Wallis Van Rijk while she was out of the Land Rover photographing those lions. I was suspended for three and a half weeks, actually. I had to work in the office in Maun. Did you know *that*?' Alix's honey-gold eyes were furious now.

'No.' It was Reed's turn to sound furious now. 'How could I have known? I've been in Zimbabwe—or had *you* forgotten?'

'Although I'm an experienced guide,' she went on, 'I was confined to the office, where I made out endless requisitions, arranged supplies and the hire of Land Rovers for *other* safaris, so to hear you joking about Miss Boyer's senseless behaviour makes me boil!'

Quite suddenly she felt dizzy and she could actually feel herself beginning to lose colour. Well, she thought, it was not surprising, since she had skipped breakfast and got herself into a rage on a baking hot day.

Reed took her arm. 'Alix? Are you all right?'

'No.' She shook her arm free. 'As it happens, Reed, I am *not* all right! I'm absolutely furious! Don't you dare joke about your girlfriend to me again!'

Ah, she thought—there, it's out. Your girl-friend. Let's face it, you're jealous that Camille Boyer is going to be in on the next safari.

'I can understand your distress,' Reed said. He honestly sounded concerned, but Alix turned and started to walk away from him. Suddenly she swung round.

'Don't give me any more bad news, OK? First I hear that you're to fly with me to Maun, and sec-ondly, I'm supposed to go into a fit of hysterical giggling over Camille being tied to the Land Rover seat. Anyway, you know the arrangements. *We're* to fly to Maun together and the other three will follow a few hours later. In the meantime, will you please brief Miss Boyer about the rules? I'll expect those rules to be adhered to. I happen to be a guide, Reed, not a baby-sitter!'

He was furious now. 'Fine, Alix. I'll pass on the message—word for word.'

She watched him for a moment as he left her and then drove off in his rented car.

After a restless night, she was on her way back to Look-Out Safaris the next morning, and, keeping to her usual routine, she parked her car in the private parking space for staff. The Land Rover, which she would pick up in Maun, she was told, had been serviced and passed A1 for the forth-coming safari.

A courtesy bus brought Reed from the Holiday Inn, and Alix greeted him briefly.

'Our courtesy bus is waiting to take us to the airport,' she said. 'I hope you'll enjoy the flight to Maun.'

He gave her one of his half-smiles. 'I see no reason why not.'

What a fool she had been to think that Reed had arranged another safari just to see her again, she thought. How naïve could she get? Reed Forsythe was nothing but a wealthy playboy, and the idea of organising another safari and paying for the entire thing himself had nothing whatsoever to do with Alix Sandton—except, perhaps, someone to amuse himself with if he had the chance.

When they were on the plane Reed said, 'I said I'd be in touch. Didn't you believe me?'

'I hadn't really given it another thought,' she answered coolly.

'Well, *give* it a thought.' His voice was curt.

'My sole purpose is to act as your guide. I am not in the habit of indulging in a relationship with any of my passengers. By the way,' Alix dropped her lashes, 'perhaps it would be in your own interest if you fastened you seat-belt, since we're about to take off.'

Losing patience with her, he said coldly, 'Have you quite finished airing your temper, Alix?'

She realised it was pointless to go on like this, and, trying to salvage the pleasure she had experienced when she had walked into Karl's office to find him there, she said, 'I'm sorry. It defeats me, though, why you should have thought I would have been over the moon to hear you joking about

Camille having got out of the Land Rover to photograph lion. I intend to drop the matter. Let's hope Camille will play the game on this safari.'

As she met Reed's eyes, Alix realised how attracted she was to him, and she knew it was dangerous to become involved with him. The idea of Camille having possibly been to bed with Reed filled her with jealousy, even though she knew very well that she had no justification to feel that way. It seemed obvious, however, that Reed was just after a good time. She reached for her bag and took out a magazine and began to read, without really knowing what she was reading about.

'By the way,' said Reed, after a while, 'this heavy silence doesn't upset me.' His expression was both amused and irritable.

'That's what I thought.' Alix smiled suddenly. 'I thought you wanted silence as much as I wanted it.'

'Why are we talking such nonsense, Alix, when all we really want to do is to get to know one another—and to make love?'

After a moment she said, 'I'm very much involved with somebody else. The last thing on my mind is having *you* make love to me.'

'He's going to have to adjust to the idea that you're going to be unfaithful to him. You and I, Alix, are going to put this safari to good use. Make up your mind to it.' There was a trace of mockery in Reed's dark blue eyes.

'Reed, I've got news for you. I'm not available.' As she spoke she felt both exhilarated and depressed.

Soon after they had touched down in Maun she said, 'Well, we'll have to part company for a while. I have to pick up the Land Rover and then the supplies for the safari, which are already waiting for me.' As their eyes met she found herself laughing a little. 'Unless you want to add to these supplies, as you did the last time—or go thirsty as the sun goes down. In other words, will you be wanting to purchase your plonk for the safari?'

'I have no intention of not safeguarding against dehydration, Alix, believe me.' A gust of wind ruffled his dark hair and he pushed his tanned fingers through it. 'I suggest, therefore, that we keep together.'

'Fine.' She decided to relax with him and to enjoy being with him.

'Another thing, Alix, when it comes to you—I'm a fighter. Make up your mind to it.'

'Maybe, but just you make up your mind that you'll definitely not be a winner—not when it comes to making it with me.'

Alix enjoyed having Reed with her as she picked up the Land Rover and the necessary supplies for the safari. They went to buy what she had light-heartedly referred to as 'plonk', and then it was time to meet the plane—and the plane meant Camille. Alix tried to shove her dismal thoughts to one side.

It was fun saying hello again to Mercedes and Hugo, but she found it difficult to greet Camille pleasantly, especially since Camille was complaining about the bumpy flight from Gaberone to Francistown and back. The flight to Maun, she emphasised, had caused her to feel ill.

Luggage was loaded into the Land Rover. Seating arrangements were politely discussed, and there were some strained moments when Camille was ushered into the back of the Land Rover, along with Hugo and Mercedes. Glaring at Reed, she demanded, 'Why is this?'

'You'll have all the space you need when it comes to taking photographs. That makes sense, doesn't it? Why sit three in front now that Jacques and Jacquetta have left us? Cone on, Camille.' Although Reed spoke lightly enough, his eyes showed annoyance.

Later he turned in his seat so that he could talk to Camille.

'Well, what did you see in Francistown?' he asked her.

'If you are so interested, why did you not come with us?' Camille answered shortly. 'If you had come, maybe you would have been able to understand what it was that stupid guide was trying to explain to us. Hugo hired a guide, by the way, although what for I do not know.'

'Francistown has quite a history, Camille.' Alix had to raise her voice over the Land Rover noises.

'It depends what *you* refer to as history, *non*? Francistown is not exactly Europe.'

Alix decided to ignore Camille's acid sarcasm.

'Well, of course, but Francistown started as a typical mining town. Actually, a mining industry had flourished in the area in prehistoric times. There were shafts and trenches—all sunk by those early miners who were probably of the Karanga tribe. They managed to extract quite a lot of gold, but, without pumps or haulage gear, they were forced to give up directly work reached water level. Years and years later, men rushed there expecting to discover vast riches. In the 1890s Francistown was quite a loud and boisterous place and there were a few stores and bars. Later, the mines closed down and the town went into a slump, but later revived as a trading, rail, administrative and communications centre.'

'I understood nothing of what the guide was rattling on about,' Camille retorted. 'It was hot and unpleasant. We were taken to look at an old hunk of iron which was, we were told, an old locomotive. The entire excursion was a waste of time and energy.'

Here we go again, thought Alix.

'Anyway, that old hunk of iron used to pull heavy trains through Botswana and Zimbabwe, transporting gold freight, coal and even cattle,' she said.

'Try not to be touchy about it, Alix,' Camille answered. 'After all, the locomotive was not used to pull the Orient Express.'

'That had to come from you, of course.' Reed shifted again in his seat. 'How about a little harmony for a change?'

At this stage of their second safari, Mercedes and Hugo were not yet excited. Perhaps Camille's attitude was responsible, thought Alix. It was with a sigh of relief that she saw the notice board reading 'Grewia Lodge 1 km'.

Except for a strikingly handsome dark man at Reception and a smattering of staff, the small lodge appeared to be deserted.

'What's this place like?' Reed asked.

'I don't really know. We haven't used it before,' Alix answered. 'As Karl pointed out, it would have been too late to make other arrangements. Too late in the day, I mean.'

'Don't be cross,' he said, very softly.

Alix bit her lip, then said, just as softly, 'I'm very cross, but I'm going to be all right.'

'I'll make it up to you.' His smile was teasing.

'Don't press your luck,' she teased back, wanting to enjoy the safari with him.

They were shown to brick and thatch bandas which had private front patios and back entrances which led into areas accommodating small refrigerators—those almost essential items for people who enjoyed sundowners, especially when on a safari. Ice always seemed to be a must.

Directly Alix entered her own banda, she was aware of the rattling and shaking noises which came from the refrigerator, which seemed to be fighting a losing battle when it came to dealing with the heat.

As she closed her door she said, 'I'm not putting up with that noise all night,' and immediately switched off the current.

A few moments later Mercedes knocked on the door and called out, 'Alix? We visit small market place, yes? You come?'

Wanting to please, Alix opened the door. 'That's a good idea, Mercedes. I'll join you in a minute.'

The market place was near to Reception, and by the time they had all walked there and had a look around, there was only time to bath and dress for dinner when they got back to their bandas. Hugo and Mercedes had arranged for carvings, basketware and bright cotton prints to be sent to La Réunion.

Dinner was served in a boma which was hung with animal skins, and Alix glanced around, hating the owners for what they had done. She also found herself resenting Reed's half impatient, half protective attitude towards Camille.

After the meal was over everybody sat around the small swimming-pool that shimmered in front of the bandas, but the heat had dropped suddenly and the air was decidedly chilly. Alix tilted her head back to see if it was going to rain, but the sky was packed with glittering stars.

'There's a super pool at our private camp, by the way.' She glanced at Reed, who was sitting next to her. 'You remembered the camp I told you about when you decided on another safari, I see.'

'I remembered more than that.' His voice was soft, but there was a hard edge to it. 'Why else do you think I'm here, Alix?'

Camille stood up. 'I'm amazed, Alix, that in your so-called profession you cannot speak French.' Her voice contained sheer spite. 'But maybe you are proficient in some other language?'

Alix felt her temper rising, but was determined to remain cool. 'I have a passion for the exotic, Camille. I speak Swahili, Ndebeli, Tswana and siSwati. Oh well, I guess it's time for bed. Reed, Mercedes, Hugo... if you'll excuse me?'

'I'll see you to your banda,' Reed said quickly.

She was going to refuse, but instead she said sweetly, 'Thank you. You're very kind, Reed.'

When they reached her door he said, 'Have a drink with me later, Alix.'

'No, thank you. Have a drink with your protégée instead.'

As she closed her door her honey-gold eyes glittered with satisfaction.

CHAPTER THREE

ALIX drew the curtains, shutting out the night, and then, feeling depression taking over from satisfaction, she began to run another bath, just for something to do.

The safari was turning out to be a disaster. Even one of the back tyres was giving cause for concern, and she was sure there was a slow leak. What was so infuriating was the fact that the Land Rover was supposed to have been checked by the time she had arrived in Maun to pick it up for the safari.

The water turned out to be tepid, so it was useless trying to relax in the bath.

Before going to bed she opened the back door and, using the torch which she always carried with her, she was able to see the Land Rover, which was parked immediately outside her banda. Her eyes brooded on the back tyre, which certainly looked soft.

It was amazing how chilly it had become after such intense heat, she thought, as she got into a short iris-patterned nightdress and matching briefs, which left little to the imagination. She looked out the mohair leg-warmers which she always popped into her holdall since the temperature at this time of year could prove to be unpredictable at night.

She was awakened by noises which she could only liken to railway shunting yards and, sitting up, she reached for the lamp switch, since the lodge was equipped with electricity throughout the night. The noises had not been imagined, and she felt herself shiver. There was nothing else for it, she would have to get out of bed to investigate. Maybe someone was tampering with the Land Rover?

It took a lot of nerve to unlock the back door and open it, but she could see nothing, as she flashed the torch. Just typical, she thought. Once she'd got up to listen and investigate the noises had stopped, so she went back to bed, although she was feeling far from happy.

She did not think she would sleep again, but, directly she became warm, she did—only to be disturbed again by the same 'shunting' noises. Her thoughts flew to the eerie motel she and her mother had stayed in when visiting Pisa. The motel was reputed to have been haunted. Was the Grewia haunted? Was that why it was so empty?

'Damn,' she said aloud, 'get a grip on yourself and see what's going on. It's probably something hilarious. A buffalo, maybe, rubbing against the bumper of the Land Rover.'

The torch beam was powerful. Alix's hand trained the beam on the Land Rover, the tyres, the walls of her banda, the walls of Reed's banda—the windows . . . other bandas. She opened the door of the Land Rover and then, without stopping to think, banged it shut.

'What the hell's going on?' called Reed as he tried to peer past the light.

'It's me—Alix.'

'Alix?' He laughed, as though he didn't believe her. 'What the devil are you doing out here?' He came towards her and she switched the torch off.

'I keep hearing noises,' she said. 'Have *you* heard noises?'

'I've been dead to the world. The only noises I've heard are the noises made by you. You've made enough noise to waken the dead, Alix, and what's the flashing torch all about?'

'Maybe my banda is haunted. I'm sure the noises were inside.'

'In that case, what are you doing, roaming about outside on your own?'

'Oh, forget it,' she said crossly, as she made for her door. 'I'm not in the mood to argue with you.'

'Look, let me investigate, Alix. It'll put your mind at rest.'

He was, she noticed when they were in her banda, wearing cotton shorts and nothing else. His tanned legs were strong and his feet, like his hands, well shaped.

'Would you like me to look in the wardrobe?' he asked, turning to look at her with something like amusement.

'Look, if you like,' Alix answered stiffly. She watched him as he opened the doors of the built-in wardrobe.

'Nothing there. No spooks.' His dark blue eyes went over her iris-embroidered nightdress and then to the ridiculously fancy leg-warmers which followed on from her short skirt. Quite suddenly the atmosphere seemed charged with his masculinity and she was aware of the powerful sexual undercurrent between them before she reached for the wrap which went with the nightdress.

'No spooks. No noise.' Obviously, she thought furiously, he's enjoying this. After a moment he said, 'What noise, Alix?'

When she made no reply he said, still in that amused voice, 'You haven't answered my question, Alix.' His eyes lingered suggestively on her hips.

'Perhaps I didn't like your question. However, there've been spells of silence when I even managed to doze off, only to be startled out of my wits again. I just can't understand it.'

'This, then, appears to be one of those—er—silent spells.' Reed went on looking at her and their eyes held, and Alix felt something like shock going right through her. The casual mockery was there again, along with the groove in one cheek.

'Don't sabotage me, Reed! You don't believe me, do you? You think I've been slamming doors and flashing the torch to waken you... I knew the noise was inside the banda, but on the other hand I couldn't be all that sure, and I had to check. It's as if someone is twisting a metal pipe out of shape and then flinging it from a height into the bath—that sort of noise. Oh, this is a total *joke*!' She took an impatient breath.

Reed laughed outright. 'Oh, come! You sound just like a hypochondriac!'

'What has a hypochondriac got to do with this?' she asked furiously. 'Why don't you just get out of here?'

'A hypochondriac, Alix, will take a small or meaningless symptom and exaggerate it.'

'Look, Reed, I'm sorry I bothered you——' she began.

'Maybe you were dreaming?' His eyes rested on her mouth.

'I was not dreaming—and what's more, forget it. I don't need your help. I'll sort this out myself. It's not the first time I've had a problem on safari.' There was an accusing silence on her part. 'You've been insulting me, and I resent that. And now will you go?'

They were still standing in the hall which accommodated the refrigerator and shelving space which was there to serve those guests who wanted to bring food into the banda. The bathroom led off the other side. Alix moved away so that she was not standing so close to Reed—then caught her breath as her feet dipped into ice-cold water. Before she could help herself, she slipped on the polished cement floor and would have fallen, had he not reached out and caught her.

Feeling more frustrated with every second, she said, 'What goes on in this place? The floor's streaming with water!'

'Here, permit me, before you fall and break that lovely neck.' He lifted her up before she could do anything about it.

'Oh, damn you, Reed, put me down!' she protested. 'This is ridiculous! I wasn't going to fall.'

He did not put her down until they were in the bedroom, and then, when he did, he did not release his hold on her. Alix noticed his long, assessing look and hated him.

'You just haven't believed a word of what I've told you, have you? Do you think *I* put the water there?' Her furious honey-gold eyes flickered over his face. 'Reed, will you take your hands off me?'

'I'm not complaining, Alix.' He laughed softly, and this made her struggle, but he held her closer to him and she could feel the heat of his body. Immediately he sought her lips, she was aware of the challenge of his kiss.

She could feel the hairs of his chest tickling her breasts through the flimsy material of her nightdress, for her robe had fallen open, and she felt electrified by this closeness. The awareness between them intensified, and she was beginning to get excited—against her will. As Reed kissed her, he moved her robe so that it slithered down to her elbows, then he eased the straps of her nightdress off her shoulders so that he could kiss and stroke them with tantalising slowness. Alix promised herself that this wouldn't happen again. It must not happen again, she thought. Just this once. His hands moved to her hips, drawing her even closer, and she began slowly to drown with longing.

He smelt clean and sexy from some special soap—certainly not the tiny scrap that graced all the soapdishes in the bathrooms of the lodge.

'You smell wonderful,' she whispered against his mouth.

He drew back to look at her, and because her eyes were closed, she failed to see the mockery in his eyes. 'The credit must go to Calvin Klein's Obsession for men—and since you're in such a generous mood, Alix, perhaps we should make ourselves more comfortable? I came back to pursue this, believe me, but it's happened much sooner than I expected.'

His remarks shocked her and brought her to her senses. As she pushed him away she said, 'Is that what you think of me? I—I just can't believe this! I want you to know that I have no experience of this sort of thing.' She slapped his face.

After a moment he said, 'I find that hard to believe, Alix. After all, you're beautiful and you appear—liberated. It seemed unlikely to me that you'd be—untouched. Isn't this just what you expected? I'm as clued up as the next man, when it comes to the...'

She cut in quickly, 'You're so clued up that you thought—the way all men think—that I invented the noises. That I slammed the door of the Land Rover and flashed the torch to attract your attention. Well, you're quite wrong!'

Reed shrugged his shoulders. 'So I was wrong. I got carried away—but then so did you. My apologies, Alix. I'll be perfectly honest—I was disappointed in you.'

'You were disappointed in me? I like that! Can you imagine any woman who's trying to make it wearing these ridiculous leg-warmers? Can you? Do I look sexy?'

'You look very sexy, make no mistake.' His eyes went over her legs.

She was seized by fury. 'Get out of my banda! I don't need your help. If need be, I'll spend the rest of the night in the Land Rover!'

Just at that moment they both heard the noises which she had likened to shunting noises.

'There!' Her voice was triumphant. 'I *told* you!'

Reed was already on his way to the small hall, and as she followed him, Alix heard him say, 'The water's coming from the refrigerator.' And then she remembered.

Feeling utterly stupid, she said, 'I've just remembered—I switched it off and now it's defrosting. Those are ice noises. The ice is falling in chunks on to the metal shelves.'

If she had not been feeling so angry she would have collapsed with laughter. Another piece of ice dislodged itself and fell with a loud metallic noise.

'Why did you disconnect it in the first place?' asked Reed. 'What was the point?'

As he spoke Alix suddenly realised that she was still without her robe, and she went to retrieve it from the floor in the other room.

When she joined him again she explained, 'The noise was getting on my nerves. The floor is probably uneven and the cabinet seemed to be rattling and dancing all over the place. I turned it off before we went to the market-place, before dinner.'

She left him to go to the bathroom for a towel, which still carried the trace of her own perfumed soap, and when she returned he was still there. 'So that's what you think of me?' She dropped the towel on the floor and stood on it. 'You believe I'm easy game—is that it? As I drive men like you on game-viewing safaris I'm easy game!' Her eyes were blazing.

'Well, let's face it, Alix, a lot of women use their sex appeal to get what they want—where they want to go.'

'And men are such pushovers when it comes to sex, aren't they? Did you think I was panting for you?'

She saw the angry glint in Reed's dark blue eyes. 'I'll be honest with you, Alix. I thought—well, if this is what the sun-goddess wants, that's just fine with me. I was wrong about you. I'm glad I was wrong. Once again, I apologise.'

'Oh, sure. You—*once again*—you've apologised. Shall I go down on my knees to thank you?' Her voice was heavy with sarcasm. 'How easy for you! I, on the other hand, am left feeling like a dissolute woman. Look, don't expect me to be nice about this. Right from the start, I summed you up as a useless playboy. I didn't need Camille to put me wise.'

'So I'm a playboy of the worst kind? Oh come, Alix. Maybe I was still half asleep.' Reed smiled suddenly. 'Look, after all this, I'm going back to pour myself a nightcap. Let me bring you something. There's been a misunderstanding. I got carried away...'

'The last thing I have on my mind, Reed, is a nightcap,' she snapped. 'And now, will you go?'

She took a long time getting to sleep again, and almost wished she had accepted his offer of a drink. Her small travelling clock reminded her, with a long impatient whine, that it was morning and time to get up.

The air was still chilly, but with the threat of heat to come. They left the Grewia Lodge soon after breakfast and Alix kept to the rough road which ran along the river. Game-viewing had begun again.

They had lunch in an open-air thorn boma and, taking care not to include Reed in the conversation, Alix pointed out a fish eagle's nest, and Camille, who was apparently also sulking with Reed, went out of her way to explain about the nest to Mercedes and Hugo.

Later, Mercedes and Camille went to freshen up, and Hugo also disappeared.

'How long is this going to last, Alix?' asked Reed, when they were alone. 'You're still pretty mad with me, aren't you?'

'It's all right.' The tone of her voice implied that it was anything but all right. 'I *was* mad, but what makes you think I'm still mad with you? Just enjoy yourself. That is what you're here for, and it's up to me to make this safari a success. I've got more to think about than last night.'

'Good.' Reed spoke angrily. 'I'm glad to hear that, although this is hardly the impression you've given me up to now.'

'All that concerns me is that *you* enjoy your safari.'

'Do you think that's why I came back, Alix? Solely to enjoy myself—game-viewing and taking photographs?'

She stood up. 'Excuse me—I want to freshen up before we get going again. We have some distance to cover before we reach the Sycamore Safari Lodge.'

By the time they reached the Sycamore Safari Lodge, the heat of the day which gathered and intensified had not abated, and as Alix parked the Land Rover she said, 'I'm quite excited about this stop. I don't often bring tourists here, since it doesn't belong to Look-Out Safaris. It's extra plush.'

'I'd read about. it,' Reed answered. 'Karl Sievewright was more than willing to arrange it.'

Camille's face was set and discontented-looking. 'Reed, the heat has got to me—Mercedes also. Maybe we should all take a rest, the moment we become settled?'

'By all means take a rest,' he answered.

'But what about you?' Her eyes went over his face.

'Never mind about me, OK? I can take good care of myself. You should know that by now.'

Alix tried not to gloat as she gave instructions regarding the luggage, which was being lifted from the Land Rover.

With its white weathered walls, corridors, crooked walks and reeds fitted into arched openings, the safari lodge created instant excitement. Unusual effects were created by narrow winding garden corridors, which had arches and roofs made of sticks. These corridors led off to the eight chalets which formed the lodge. A pool with an intricate mosaic design glittered beneath the sun and there were crimson sun-umbrellas on roof-gardens and next to the pool. Pink and crimson bougainvillaea seemed to add to the exciting atmosphere, along with brick-paved sidewalks and big flowerpots.

Not long after everybody was settled in Reed came to the door of Alix's chalet, and since it was open, he called out, 'Your camera, Alix. You left it in the Land Rover.'

'You needn't have bothered, but thank you.' She took the camera from him and turned away. When she had placed the camera on the cane bedside table she looked up and saw that he was still standing there.

'You look tired, Alix,' he said softly.

Her shoulders ached, and as she stared moodily at him, she began to massage the back of her neck with her fingertips.

'Well, I'm not. Reed, is that all? Just the camera?'

'No, it's not all. When I got to Zimbabwe, I couldn't get you out of my mind.'

'That's one problem I can't solve for you. I'd like to take a shower now, so you'll have to excuse me.'

He'd never know, she thought, how attracted she was to him. What was more, she would see to it that he didn't ever get to know.

By late afternoon, everybody confessed to feeling refreshed and ready for more game-spotting, and as Alix strode to the Land Rover on long slender legs, she looked like a high-fashion model in her immaculate safari trouser suit.

The moment Reed got in beside her, she became conscious of his body and the way in which his arms had pressed her to him the night before. As she backed out of the small parking area, she imagined herself making love with him, beneath the soaring thatched roof of her chalet. She was also aware that his eyes were on her, and for his ears alone, she said, 'It makes me nervous when you stare at me like that.' She turned to look at him briefly.

'Why should you be nervous?' he asked.

'Because I've decided to have an attack of nerves, that's why. In other words, I'm having an attack of—is-everything-going-to-be-all-*wrong*-on-this-safari? It's not a nice feeling and I'm not in a very good mood.'

'In that case, join the club, Alix,' Reed answered shortly. 'I'm not in a very good mood either.'

In the back of the Land Rover, Mercedes and Hugo were beginning to relax and show their excitement as they scanned the bush for wild animals. So far as they were concerned, the spirit of the safari was suddenly revived.

There was excitement on the way back to the lodge as a huge elephant lumbered out of the riverine forest and began to walk in the centre of the rough road. Since she had the river bank on one side and huge ditches and potholes on the other, Alix had no intention of trying to pass him.

Excitement on the part of her passengers gave way to nervous tension as the elephant decided to take his time, and as he swayed from one side of the road to the other, he appeared to be quite intoxicated. This could have been hilarious, had there not been a danger element.

'He must have been eating marula fruit,' said Alix, glancing at Reed. 'When the fruit ferments, it becomes a good producer of alcohol, so they say, and animals—and even birds—enjoy the aromatic fruit. Bull elephants have appeared to be quite drunk after eating it.'

'An elephant would have to consume masses of fruit, I should imagine, to reach that stage, but it certainly looks as if this one has been on the tiles all afternoon.' Reed's manner was mocking, and Alix had the feeling he was waiting for her to make her first mistake when it came to dealing with the problem of getting past the animal.

Eventually the elephant left the road and made for the bush and trees which grew on the banks of the river. As the Land Rover rattled and shook past him, he put his head back, lifted his trunk and flapped his ears. Into the bargain, his mouth was wide open, which caused Camille and Mercedes to shriek with fright.

Feeling elated now, Alix began to laugh. 'Wow! Wasn't that thrilling?' She turned to look at Reed. 'Thank goodness he didn't turn and charge us! This is what a safari is all about.'

'Nice work,' he answered, but she was quick to notice the trace of mockery in his dark blue eyes. 'You're very capable, Alix.'

'I'm glad you're getting the idea.' A smile lurked at the corners of her lips. 'That manic elephant just made our day!'

As they reached the lodge Reed said, 'We'll see you at dinner.' Beneath his smile Alix could sense his anger. He had not forgiven her for slapping his face, she thought.

'I don't think so. I expect there'll be somebody here I know.'

'Alix, how long is this going to carry on?' He gave her a glance of acute annoyance. 'I'll expect you to have dinner with us.'

'I can't think why,' she retorted. 'Most people hate pushy guides.' She felt stifled and restless. 'I told you that before.'

'Well, I'm not "most people". I'll call for you. There's nothing pushy about this.'

Before she began to walk in the direction of her chalet she gave him an impatient glance. 'There'll be no need to call for me—I'll meet you at Reception.'

Much to her annoyance, Camille ran to catch up with her. 'One moment, Alix!'

'What is it?' Alix turned.

'You are far too ambitious. If you are hoping to get somewhere with Reed Forsythe, I am afraid you will not get that chance. Do not say I did not warn you,' Camille said nastily.

Alix felt her temper rising. 'I have no patience with petty spite, Camille. That's the kind of remark I find myself shrinking from. Don't get any big ideas about me with Reed.' Deliberately she changed direction and went towards the path which led to the reception desk—only to discover Reed there. He was looking at some postcards and when he saw her he said,

'I was just thinking how well a drink would go down before showering. Will you join me?'

There was a pause in which Alix thought, to hell with Camille!

'I'd like that. Where?'

'On my patio.' His eyes mocked her. 'When you can't lick them, join them. Eh, Alix?'

She gave him one of her honey-gold stares.

'Oh, *I* wouldn't say that.'

Ten minutes later she was holding her hand out to him as he passed her a shandy. Camille chose that moment to join them, and Alix felt her nerves going taut.

'What about me?' Camille's eyes went to Reed's glass. 'I am parched!'

Alix noticed Camille's moody eyes watching Reed as he poured her a drink and handed it to her. As she accepted it she said, 'I came, Alix, to show you a photograph of Reed's château. I am sure you will like to see it, *non*? I have it here, in my bag. You remember the one, Reed—the one which I took of you and—*Theresa?*'

'I'm afraid I don't.' He was abrupt.

'In that case, permit me to refresh your memory.'

Alix, sensing something, watched tensely as Camille took an envelope, containing several photographs, from her brightly woven bag.

The turreted château, she saw, was shrouded in ivy. Reed and a stunningly beautiful girl were standing in front of the arched entrance, into which was fitted a heavy door, studded with shining brass nail-heads.

'As you can see, Alix,' Camille's light laughter sounded false, 'we *both* have a rival. Theresa is very beautiful, is she not, Reed?'

'All women who figure in my life are beautiful. By the way, I don't think we want to see the others, so you can put them away and we can enjoy our drinks.'

'As you have obviously guessed, Alix, Reed is immensely rich,' Camille said spitefully.

'If he is, I dare say he earned it.' Alix put her glass down and stood up. 'Thank you for the drink, Reed. I always seem to be saying that, don't I? I'll see you later.'

A few moments later she was stepping into a bath, and as she stretched out in the bubbly water she brooded on the photograph, and Camille's remarks. When she thought of what Reed had said—

all women who figure in my life are beautiful—she felt depressed beyond description. She realised that if she did not treat this as any other safari, she was scheduled for a disaster.

She looked out narrow khaki cotton trousers and the shoulder-strapped white embroidered camisole she had worn on the day that Reed had come into her life again. The camisole emphasised her tan, and to add the usual touch of glamour she decided to wear her gold hooped earrings and a chunky gold bracelet. The bracelet gleamed against her skin and did things for her wrist, which was slender and small-boned.

Reed, she was quick to notice as she walked into the reception area and saw him standing there with Hugo, Mercedes and Camille, was wearing white canvas trousers and a royal blue shirt which seemed to draw attention to the colour of his incredible blue eyes. Her eyes strayed to his mouth, which was sensual without appearing in the least soft. This wealthy, bearded and moustached playboy could have a very disrupting effect on her life, she thought.

They went through to the dining-room and were shown to a long table. Darkness had closed in on the Sycamore Safari Lodge, and as the limited number of visitors dined in the exciting space they were all aware of the fact that the lodge was surrounded by such wild animals as elephant, lion, hyena and cheetah, to name but a few. Conversation throughout the meal was difficult, since the French couple from the island of La Réunion could only speak to Camille and Reed, and for the fact that tension seemed to have settled upon Alix, Reed and Camille. The name 'Theresa' hung like a thread between them.

After the meal was over, Alix excused herself and went straight to her chalet, where she sat brooding on the patio. She jumped a little when Reed surprised her.

'Come and walk, Alix.' It sounded like an order, not an invitation. Being in charge of this safari was like fighting to stay in one piece, she thought.

'There's no place to walk,' she answered shortly. '*You* know that!'

He reached for her hand and drew her up beside him. 'Come to the wall to listen to the animal noises.'

Trying to appear only politely interested, she shrugged. 'OK, if that's what you want.'

'It is what I want.' His eyes searched hers in the light of the lantern which was suspended from the wall.

They went to stand next to the alarmingly low wall, which was topped by a wooden railing. There was an element of danger about being here that quickened the senses.

'There's so much I want to know about you,' Reed said softly.

After a moment Alix said, 'It isn't a big secret. I have a very well ordered and private life. I told you about my cottage last time.'

'But you take a lot of risks—your job alone. Your private life can't be all well ordered and private.'

'I don't take risks. I live alone. You don't believe that, do you?'

'It's what I want to believe.'

'Really?' Her voice was sarcastic as she thought about the girl named Theresa and the countless other women, beautiful—all beautiful, he'd said—who figured in his life.

'Yes, really.'

In the star-spangled darkness she anticipated his touch and watched him as he reached for her and sought her lips with his own. She was aware of the growing desire between them, and then the frantic excitement she was feeling began to struggle with reluctance. Excitement won, and she found herself clinging to him.

'I love you,' said Reed softly. 'God, Alix, I want you! I've thought of nothing else since we parted that first time.'

The same old thing: I want you, Alix.

She broke away from him. 'Don't try to use me, Reed! I'm not prepared for that. I'm not just off the boat and I am, I hope, far too wise, far too intelligent to fall for—"I love you, Alix. I want you, Alix." Just leave me alone, will you?'

As she left him and ran in the direction of the chalets she thought that nothing like this had happened to her before—where she was so *tempted*.

CHAPTER FOUR

THE PROBLEM of the leaking tyre had to be sorted out, Alix thought, and decided to skip breakfast so that she could drive to the small workshop before she embarked on another game-viewing safari.

When she got to the workshop, she was informed that she would have to come back later, since there was no one there at the moment who carried the authority to supervise the changing and repairing of tyres.

Later, as she explained the position to Reed, he waited until she was finished and then he said, 'You weren't at breakfast. Why?' His voice carried an authority which she resented.

'I didn't feel like breakfast. To get to the point, though—maybe you would all enjoy a swim? The pool looks heavenly. By that time the Land Rover problems will have been sorted out.'

'The others can please themselves what they want to do. I'll go with you to the workshop.' Their eyes held and Alix expelled an impatient breath.

'There'll be no need for you to go to the workshop, Reed. I want to get this problem sorted out without a whole lot of fuss. It's maddening enough as it is.'

'If there does happen to be a whole lot of fuss, Alix, you're the one who's creating it. I'll explain what's happening to the others and I'll join you in a few moments.'

As he turned to leave her she called out, 'Don't you understand *anything*?'

She had made up her mind to go without him, but he arrived just as she was getting into the Land Rover.

'I'm used to snags on a safari,' she told him, as he slammed the door shut.

'I too am used to snags. Pipe down, Alix, for God's sake!' Reed's eyes looked even darker when he was annoyed, she thought, and felt something like a thrill.

Although it was early in the morning, the heat was becoming oppressive, and as she stood around and fumed, Alix envied Mercedes, Hugo and Camille, who would probably be in the sun-glittered pool.

Because of the heat, Reed had begun to unbutton his shirt, and her eyes went to his bare chest and she felt her pulse quicken. He lifted his lashes to look at her.

'Well, Alix? What are you brooding about now?'

'I'm not brooding, but you are supposed to be making the best of your safari. Don't ever push me into saying this again, Reed, but I'm here to do my job while *you* sit back and enjoy yourself. This is what you've paid for.'

'Who says I'm *not* enjoying myself? I wanted to see for myself that the tyres are checked. After all, our safety depends on them.' He spoke more in amusement than in anger, but Alix felt her temper flare.

'And of course, coming from France, you're an expert on Land Rovers and the African bush and swamps, is that it?'

Reed was clearly losing patience now. 'I'm more expert than you think. There seems to be some confusion in your mind about me, Alix.'

'Don't you think that a woman can be efficient enough to see to it that tyres are checked and repaired efficiently?' she demanded.

'Just say that I'd feel a whole lot better if *I* supervised what's going on here.' To prove his point he left her to involve himself with the matter in hand while Alix stared at him, too angry to follow him.

When he joined her again she said, 'I'd like to get something else straight. I have no wish to be swept off my feet by you, or any other man I happen to be driving round the game reserve. I enjoy my work as a guide. Most of the time, that is. I enjoy certain benefits, but sharing my bed at night is not one of them. I'm referring to what happened last night, of course. You remember your position on this safari, and I'll remember mine. This, by the way, is the advice of a competent, experienced guide.' Her honey-gold eyes narrowed. 'What *did* you expect of me last night, by the way? I'd like to know.'

'Well, Alix, since you want to know, I'll tell you. But first of all, I do know what to expect of *myself*, and when a girl kisses me back the way *you* kissed me last night, I've got to go as far as I can with her. Satisfied?' Reed was smiling now and spoke with a deliberately brutal carelessness. 'I'm too much of an expert not to have recognised the desire in you.'

'I admit I might have been carried away, but I do not share the male point of view about—physical needs,' she answered.

'No?' The groove in his cheek deepened.

'No!'

'I believe that the average woman today, Alix, takes a very positive step towards her physical needs. I don't think you're all that different.'

Alix stared back at him, stunned. 'Take my advice,' she said after a moment, 'just don't try to turn me on again. I can tell you here and now, it won't turn out the way you envisage.'

'For God's sake, Alix, you're as aware as I am of what's happened between us. What are we wasting time for?'

Alix turned away furiously and then went to sit on a nearby tree stump and watched, without really seeing anything, as the spare tyre to the Land Rover was being tested for air. Finally the vehicle was ready to be driven away and Reed had decided to handle tipping the men who had been involved in the work himself, while Alix handled the charge, since the account would go through Look-Out Safaris.

When they were back in the Land Rover Alix said, 'It's been over an hour.'

'You'll feel a whole lot better, knowing the fault has been sorted out,' Reed replied.

'Meaning because *you* were there to see to it?'

'Oh, come, Alix! Enough is enough.'

'I have one or two things to attend to and then I'll meet you all in the curio shop,' she said stiffly, 'and by the way, I'm sorry about all this. The tyres should have been thoroughly checked at Maun. I intend submitting a report to that effect.'

He shrugged his shoulders. 'No problem. Forget it.'

By the time Alix went into the curio shop, she was still not in the best of moods, and she swore softly as she saw Camille approaching her.

'You are very good at trying to organise people, Alix, are you not?'

'Thank you. How beautifully you express that, Camille. I'm flattered.' Alix did not sound flattered. She sounded, as she felt, furious.

'But you must have misunderstood, Alix. I did not mean it as a compliment.'

'You don't have to explain, I know what you meant. You meant it as an insult. Right?'

'Oh, and one thing more, Alix, Reed is a very calculating man. He is as calculating at ending an affair as he is at starting it—I should know. Your day will come.'

'You appear to be having difficulty in growing up,' Alix retorted.

'Believe me, Alix, I have your best interests at heart.'

'Oh, I'm sure you have, Camille, just as long as those interests happen to coincide with the interests of Miss Boyer.'

Alix began to move away, but Camille followed her and then, swinging round, Alix said, 'I don't want to pursue this. When will you get it into your head that I'm not interested in Reed Forsythe? I'm here as your safari guide, nothing more. To put your mind at rest, I happen to have a good relationship with a man in Gaberone.'

Camille's laugh was spiteful. 'A good relationship? I hear those words all the time. Who doesn't? Those words are used to describe an affair, *non*? An affair, as we all know, can be quite long, or on the other hand, an affair can be confined to a matter of a few days. Is that what you are hoping for with Reed? Well, forget it. If you are hoping that a few days will lengthen into a lifetime, you are mistaken. With Reed, it means nothing. At this present time in history, put it down to the hot African sun and the romantic African moon and the wild animals who enjoy wild love. That is all it means to him. Reed has a commitment in France.'

After giving Camille a long, penetrating look, Alix turned away and made her way to the terrace which led off the curio shop and overlooked the river. Beneath a thatched umbrella, Mercedes and Hugo were sitting at a table for two. Mercedes lifted her glass of sparkling orange juice. 'It is nice, Alix. You drink?'

'I'm longing for a glass.' Alix did her best to sound cheerful and relaxed as she sat down at a table for four. It was feasible that when Reed and Camille appeared on the scene they should join her, and Alix realised that, if the safari was to be a success, she would have to shove her feelings to one side.

Looking across at Reed, she said pleasantly enough, 'Shall we leave in about ten minutes?'

'That will be fine,' he replied curtly, and she found herself wondering where the relaxed feeling they had enjoyed at Maun together had flown to. Suddenly enjoying one another's company, they had picked up the Land Rover and the supplies and then gone to buy Reed's 'plonk' for the safari.

As they left the lush vegetation of the river banks to go game-spotting the harsh terrain ahead appeared strangely beautiful in its own way, wrapped as it was in the heat haze. From time to time, Alix's eyes went to Reed's tanned hands. They were, she kept reminding herself, the hands of a man who knew how to caress a woman with skilful understanding. He had admitted he took what he could. It seemed obvious that Camille had known the feel of these hands and that those separate tents on the previous safari, and the 'single' accommodation, which was booked for them on this safari, counted for very little. As Reed lost interest in Camille, he had organised that she should sit in the back of the Land Rover while he occupied the front with Alix.

Lunch, which had been prepared and packed into a hamper by the Sycamore Safari Lodge, was enjoyed in an authorised picnic area, and then, feeling refreshed and in the mood for more game-spotting,

Alix and her passengers got back into the dust-coated Land Rover. The vehicle rattled and shook over the potholes, humps and clumps of coarse grass of a vast plain with stunted bush.

'We're heading for the river and then we'll work our way back to the lodge,' said Alix, 'and by the way, this will be elephant territory—so look out!'

As usual, Mercedes and Hugo became excited over even the smallest animal, especially warthogs. For Alix's benefit Reed translated. 'Hugo says their tails remind them of radio aerials.'

'Hugo and Mercedes make wonderful passengers,' Alix answered. 'I've loved having them on this safari.'

Reed turned to look at her. 'Meaning that two others who shall remain nameless do not make wonderful passengers?'

'If the cap fits . . . Anyway, they're so easy to get along with, apart from the fact that I'm not able to converse with them in French.'

'You'll have to learn. In France, it's essential,' he answered, and, not sure what he was driving at, she kept quiet and gave her full attention to easing the Land Rover through a deep ditch which could not be avoided and which, she found herself thinking vaguely, was almost large enough to be called a ravine.

'Yes, I suppose it is essential,' she agreed, after a few moments. 'I'll think of putting it together—learning a smattering of French, at least, when and if the time comes. The chances are that I'll visit La

Réunion one of these days. Maybe I should contact your friend Armand le—what was it again?'

'Leclerc. I usually rent one of his chalets when I go to La Réunion. They're very nice. You'd like them.'

For a few moments Alix had difficulty in handling the Land Rover, which suddenly seemed to have taken on a life and a will of its own.

'Don't you find all this nerve-racking?' Reed asked.

'I'm used to it,' she told him carelessly. 'Why? Are you finding it nerve-racking?'

'I'd feel better if I were driving.' She realised he was mocking her.

'What man doesn't feel that way?' Her voice was stiff with sarcasm. 'But don't think you've succeeded in deflating me. You'd love that, wouldn't you?'

He laughed, and when she turned to look at him, he stroked the perfect line of his jaw which the new and neatly-trimmed beard accentuated.

'Let's change the subject before I blow another valve. Tell me, if I decide to holiday on the island could I rent one of Armand's chalets?' she asked.

'I'm sure you could. That's what they're there for.'

'Many of the beaches there, so I've been told, are black, caused by lava from the volcano. Do these chalets overlook a beach, and if so, what's the beach like?' Alix asked.

'Well...the beach has everything from palm trees waving their fronds to a long stretch of silvery sand.

It's protected by a coral reef. Nearby is a well equipped little port. It's pleasant to walk there, in fact, from the chalets along the sand.'

'Where *is* the port?' she asked, mainly to make conversation. It was wonderful to feel at ease with Reed again.

'St Gilles. Maybe you'll enjoy sail-surfing. It's easy for beginners in the lagoon. Experts, of course, prefer the open sea. It's a favourite sport from the beaches of St Gilles.'

'Well, I'm definitely going.' Her voice was flippant. 'Maybe I *will* enjoy sail-surfing, and maybe I'll make it to the open sea.'

The river was in sight at last. 'We may be in for some hair-raising thrills soon,' Alix said cheerfully.

'Well, let's see what you can do.' The mockery was there again, but this time she felt no resentment.

'Is that a dare, Reed?'

'For sure it's a dare.'

They were approaching a dip which curved suddenly upwards. In a situation like this, elephants were always Alix's worst fear, and when she saw them she felt the usual nervous tension. She slackened speed, then stopped the Land Rover, with the engine still running.

The elephants were negligently pushing bushes out of their way. In the group there were both males and females, and Alix was quick to notice that a calf was pressing itself against its mother.

'Why are you stopped, Alix?' Camille called out, from behind. 'At times I find you excessively without adventure—but I should not overlook the fact that I am not as old as you.'

Why was it that this girl seemed to know instinctively how to annoy her? Alix thought.

'Or as smart, Camille, when it comes to elephants.'

Camille had taken off her designer sunglasses and had her Pentax lightweight precision binoculars raised to her eyes.

'Drive up to them, Alix. They're quite oblivious to us. We all want to take photographs.'

In fact, the elephants did appear indifferent, as they flapped their ears and waved their trunks. Alix watched as the mother shoved the calf along with her trunk, then made a trumpeting sound, her ears raised. Quite suddenly another cow uprooted a bush.

By this time Mercedes and Hugo, in their ignorance, were voicing their opinions in no uncertain terms, cameras just ready to go into action.

'Please explain to them, Reed, that elephants are often quite unpredictable and cantankerous, especially when they're with a calf or calves.' Alix's voice carried quiet authority. 'Since when have they become authorities on bush-bashing, anyway?'

She was preparing for the fact that she might well have to start reversing—then shock raced through her as the bull elephant, which had started moving slowly in their direction, quickened his pace. This too was usual, but when he charged suddenly, adrenalin poured through Alix. In her mind's eye she saw the Land Rover in pieces on the ground—

herself and her passengers flattened. Dear God, I've left it too late, she thought. Her panic lasted only an instant then she was racing backwards over humps and ditches, small bushes and clumps of coarse grass, and then, having given sufficient vent to his rage, the elephant lost interest in the vehicle, but as he made for the side of the track, he immediately set about pushing over a tree. What was so funny to Alix right at this moment was the fact that several baboons sat nearby, placidly scratching one another.

'Wow!' Alix pushed her fingers through her hair as she began laughing. 'How was that for thrills?' She was loving her triumph and turned to look at her passengers in the back of the Land Rover. 'Oh, no! What are Camille and Mercedes doing on the floor? What about those photographs?'

Her honey-gold eyes were glittering with fun as she glanced at Reed, and she saw his look of appraisal.

'How was that?' she asked.

'You probably haven't failed to notice, Alix, but I've gone as white as a ghost. I felt as if I was nearing the end of my life on the oldest continent in the world.'

'Oh, come,' she teased. 'It wasn't as bad as that.'

'I have this—er—*thing* about being inconvenienced by elephants.' He was full of boyish charm and she realised that he was not altogether joking, and she enjoyed this moment with him, loving him—especially as peace, if only temporarily, reigned in the back of the Land Rover.

'I can see I've stunned my bush-bashing experts in the back,' she said softly.

The sun was red and preparing to sink through a thin gauze which clung to the horizon by the time they got back to the Sycamore Safari Lodge.

'I'll expect you on my patio for drinks, Alix,' said Reed.

She was on the point of refusing, but on second thoughts, she thought, why not?

'That will be super. I'll be with you in a few moments.' Her smile was slow and beautiful and, for a moment, her eyes rested on his mouth.

He was waiting for her when she went along to his patio.

'So, bush-basher, what's it to be?' His eyes went over her.

'I'd love a whisky and soda, right now.'

He gave her a mocking glance. 'To settle your nerves?'

'Oh, come on...what nerves?' she laughed lightly.

'I'll be honest with you, Alix, I thought I was going to end up by being a permanent part of the Chobe Game Reserve this afternoon.'

'Maybe next time,' she teased. 'I'll see what I can do. You seem to have trouble accepting that a woman guide is as capable of handling an elephant charge as any man, Reed. You didn't seriously think I was going to flap, did you? You certainly have a way of making me feel great.'

'You were great. You *are* great. I adore you,' he answered, as he poured her drink. 'Why don't you let me prove it?'

She remained silent, and then as he handed her a glass he said, 'It's not exactly Waterford, I'm afraid. One thing in its favour—it was cheap.' Alix had been with him when he had bought glasses, for the safari, in Maun. He went on, 'They'll be abandoned at the end of the safari. By that time they will have served their purpose.'

Glancing down at the glass, which was actually quite pretty, she thought, and if I'm dumb enough to succumb to your devastating charms, I too will be discarded like the cheap glasses which you bought in a small frontier town called Maun. Her mind flashed to Camille, who apparently had served her purpose and was now relegated to the back seat of the Land Rover.

Reed sat down opposite Alix and watched her through thick black lashes. His eyebrows, she noticed, were silky and well shaped. She couldn't resist saying, 'You were cut out to wear a beard.'

He touched his fingers to it. 'I'm enjoying it, actually.'

There was a silence, then he said, 'In many ways, this work must be hard on you. There's always a strong element of danger, and the terrain is rough going.'

'I love it when there's an element of danger. Apart from everything, it's always marvellous to get away from things for a while.'

'What kind of things?'

'Well, you just have to look around.' Alix lifted her glass. 'There's the rush and the rat-race, the destruction. For instance, even in small towns beautiful old buildings are being constantly bull-dozed to make way for hideous supermarkets, fancy shopping malls and even highways. Lovely old houses are being flattened to the ground.'

'Is that what made you buy your cottage? To rescue it from the bulldozers?' Reed sounded amused, and she laughed.

'Oh, come! The cottage wasn't as bad as that, and it's lovely now. I'm enjoying it.'

'When you're there, you mean?'

'You sound like Gerald,' she answered without thinking, then turning to look away she caught her breath. 'And talk of the devil...!' She felt a be-wildered fury as she saw Gerald coming along the open outdoor corridor that led to Reed's chalet. He carried the jacket to his light business suit over his shoulder, and already he was rolling back the cuffs of his shirt. Alix could hardly believe her eyes.

'Just in time,' he was saying easily. 'Are you going to take pity on me and offer me one of those?' His ice-blue eyes went to their glasses. 'What a hell of a flight! I could use a drink. Into the bargain, the touchdown was no picnic. The Cessna Stationaire just seemed to hit the airstrip. Well, Alix, don't look so stunned.'

'I don't believe this. What are *you* doing here?' Alix asked.

'What do you think I'm doing here? But since you deem it necessary to ask, dear heart, I'm not here to do an article for a wildlife magazine. Aren't you going to introduce me to my benefactor?' Gerald glanced at Reed, who was looking out another glass from a cool-aid bag.

'This is Reed Forsythe.' Alix tried to keep the rage from her voice. 'Reed—Gerald Phipps, from Gaberone.'

'The man in your life?' Reed's voice had an edge to it as he handed Gerald a glass.

'So I *am* in the picture?' Gerald matched that edge with an edge of his own. Turning to Alix, he went on, 'So this is the total sum of your ambition—which keeps us apart for *long* spells at a time?' He glanced around. 'A plush safari lodge. Game-viewing in that godforsaken scrubland and coming back at sunset to all this stucco, thick arches, patios, courtyards...you name it, to sip drinks with some handsome guy I know nothing about? Well, well!'

Trying to mask her fury, Alix said, as casually as she could, 'I was just leaving, as it happens. I'll finish my drink in my chalet, Reed, and I promise to return the glass.' She gave him a smile, and for a moment, his dark blue eyes locked with hers.

'I'll be with you in a few minutes,' Gerald called after her as she turned to leave.

He turned up about fifteen minutes later and she turned on him furiously. 'How did you know where to find me?' she demanded.

'Don't have hysterics, Alix. Actually, I walked out on a conference—just like that.' He snapped his fingers. 'I'd suddenly had enough. I found out from Maggie where you'd be at this particular stage of your safari. The rest was comparatively easy, as it happened. I was able to hitch a ride on a chartered plane—Maggie's help again. I have to leave again in the morning, but I hope all the trouble will have been worth it.'

Alix took a calming breath. 'But *why* did you come?'

'Why?' His expression was hard.

'Yes, *why?*'

'I came to find out what the bloody bush and swamps have that I haven't, that's why. I'm beginning to see, though.' He made a vague gesture in Reed's chalet's direction.

'Really? Well, you're barking up the wrong tree. Gerald, did you expect me to be over the moon at seeing you turning up here? You're interfering with my work, for God's sake!'

'I'm interfering with more than that, it would appear.' His tone was nasty.

'Another thing,' Alix went on, 'this lodge is fully—*but fully*—booked. Where exactly do you expect to sleep? This isn't exactly some vast Holiday Inn. What's more, I happen to be leaving this safari lodge at the crack of dawn tomorrow, and I don't need a whole lot of complications.'

'Maggie said you were booked into a two-bedded chalet.'

Alix flung up her hands. 'Oh, great! And don't talk about Maggie to me. She's in for a piece of my mind when I get back, believe me! If you're expecting to sleep here, go to hell! You got here. You make your own plans.'

'What plans? You've already said the place is full. I believe you. It's what I expected, anyway. So where do I spend the night, Alix? In the bush?'

'In the bush, if you like. Sleep in the plane on the airstrip, for all I care.' She felt depression descending on her. 'Damn you, Gerald! You've succeeded in making a fool of me in front of Reed Forsythe, who happens to have organised and paid for this entire safari. I'm supposed to be sharing their table tonight. As it is, I feel so ruffled now I can't see myself *having* dinner. I'd better go and explain now, before I become even more involved and at a disadvantage.'

Reed's light was on when she got there, and she could see into the room, which was very much like her own. Wearing nothing but a big towel knotted low on his hips, he came to the door. Obviously he had just showered and his dark hair was wet.

'I've come to let you know that I'll probably be having dinner with Gerald...' Alix began to say, when he cut in.

'Probably?'

'Well, *if* I eat... I just wanted to let you know.'

'I see.' She saw the coldness in his expression. 'Well, it's not serious, Alix. Tomorrow, though, will be a very different matter. I didn't pay to have your—er—friend following us around the Chobe.'

'That's not very likely to happen, Reed, but permit me to point out that I'm here merely to drive you and your party about and to supply you with interesting details about the game reserve while we're game-viewing. What I choose to do in my *free time* has nothing whatsoever to do with you.'

'Alix is correct.' Camille surprised them by coming towards the door. 'What are you going on about, Reed? One does not have to be joking when one says Alix is merely our—driver.' Camille emphasised the word driver, drawing it out insultingly. 'It is better this way. That we all go our separate ways. There is much less friction. Basically, what I am trying to say is that there is no need for Alix to be with us *all* the time.'

'Allow me to handle my own affairs,' Reed snapped.

Anxious to terminate this hideous scene, Alix said quickly, 'I'll see you in the morning.'

A few moments later she was saying to Gerald, 'This safari is turning out to be nothing but a disaster!'

'Has anything happened between you and this guy?' he asked.

Alix stared back at him. 'What are you talking about?'

Gerald was doing up the top button of his shirt and then he adjusted his tie. He reached for his jacket and shrugged his arms into the sleeves. Suddenly Alix noticed that his overnight bag was standing to one side of the cane dressing-table, which meant that he must have been to her chalet before she and Reed had noticed him.

'Let's just say I sense an awareness between you.' Gerald lifted his eyes to look at her.

'You can get that bag out of here,' she said angrily.

'Oh, come on, Alix. We're not exactly strangers. It's not as if there was only a double bed. I'm starving! Let's go along to the dining-room, where we can talk.'

'We can talk here,' she answered. 'Besides, what is there to talk about? I've said *no*!'

'While we're there, I'll *beg* for other accommodation,' said Gerald carelessly.

In the end they walked along the numerous arched corridors that led to the dining-room. The main building was beautifully set out with white weathered walls, which formed the background to ceramic murals, ferns, cycads and colourful, trimmed-back bougainvillaea.

When they spoke to Milton Ross, who was casually dressed in the khaki gear of a game warden, they were rather curtly informed that it was impossible to accommodate Gerald—unless he shared the chalet with Alix.

'It was crazy to come up here without booking.' He shrugged. 'So it's up to you.'

He looked at Alix and then, after he had walked away, she said angrily, 'I can't understand you, Gerald. What's more, I can't understand Maggie for telling you I'd be here. She knows I was in Karl's bad books only a short time ago. What are you trying to do to me?'

'Karl knows nothing about this. Be your age, Alix! I didn't exactly come here to rape you.'

Alix shut her eyes in frustration. When she opened them she said, 'Right now I could kill you, honestly! You'd better go along to Reception and explain that you'll be spending the night in chalet four so that they can have your account ready for you first thing in the morning. I'm so cross, I feel ill. This is not one of Look-Out Safaris' stopovers, and if I'm responsible for creating a problem here, it could be the last.'

She would not speak to him during dinner, although he went out of his way to talk to her. This, Alix realised, was for Reed's benefit, and she was aware of Reed's eyes on her from time to time as he dined with Camille, Mercedes and Hugo at a nearby table.

Later, in her chalet, Gerald tried to take her in his arms, and Alix snapped furiously, 'Take your hands off me, Gerald! I'll never forgive you for turning up here!'

One thing led to another and they continued to argue long after they had closed the door to her chalet, and then, tired out, they were both in a deep sleep when Reed came knocking at the door. Gerald was the first to stir and Alix heard him say, 'Blast it!'

Getting out of bed, he went to get a towel and, knotting it about his hips, he went to the door.

'Gerald?' Alix's voice was groggy from lack of sleep. 'Is anything wrong?'

'I'm sorry,' Reed was saying, 'I seem to be interrupting something, but I understood we were leaving here at six-thirty and,' there was a pause, 'it's now *eight*-thirty.'

In her bed, Alix covered her face with her hands and groaned.

'Is that right?' Gerald answered carelessly. He sounded frankly amused. 'Well, one way and another, we've had a busy night. So I'm afraid your guide is still in bed. Anyway, give her fifteen minutes or so. She'll want to shower and have something to eat, I should imagine. Is that right, honey?'

Alix thumped her pillow.

'I'm afraid I don't seem to share the amusement.' Reed's accent was precise. 'I am, after all, finding it hard to keep up with the changes in my itinerary.'

'Well, I guess you can work that one out with Alix. And now, if you'll excuse me, I have to get to the airstrip, and between Alix and me, this room looks like the beach at low tide.' Gerald laughed lightly. 'We've got some tidying up to do.'

Alix kept her eyes on him as he came back from the door. 'What are you trying to *do* to me?' she asked furiously.

He laughed outright. 'Don't look so mad. It was just a little harmless fun.'

'Yes—a little harmless fun, at my expense. Look, I want to use the bathroom first. I'm in a mad hurry. We were supposed to have left for our private Marula Game Lodge two hours ago.' She reached for her kimono, and as she lifted her long legs from the bed, she slipped her arms into its wide silken folds and stood up.

While she dressed, Gerald showered, then Alix packed hurriedly, and although she had spent a lot of the night bickering with Gerald, she was the epitome of chic in a fresh khaki outfit. Her honey-gold eyes were clear and her dark auburn hair sleek and shining. As always, she was simply and effortlessly beautiful.

She was on the patio when Gerald came out of the room. He was wearing his pale grey three-piece business suit, which emphasised his fairness and his unusual ice-blue eyes.

Turning, she asked, 'Where will you be going now?'

'After breakfast, back home. Where else? I left my car in Maun. I can't say I'm looking forward to taking off in that small plane again.' He glanced at his watch. 'What's more, I was told I had to be on time. Are you coming to breakfast?' Their eyes met.

'No. I'll have to skip breakfast.'

'Are you going to forgive me?' His voice was soft. He leaned over and kissed her. 'That's for the benefit of your client. I'll be seeing you, Alix.'

He picked up his bag and, feeling frustrated, Alix reached for her own which was on the patio table. Her Gucci leather bag hung from her shoulder. She knew that Reed had witnessed the kiss through one of the reeded arches. Camille was with him, and for once, she looked pleased with life.

On her way to the Land Rover Alix said, 'Reed, I'm sorry. I'll make up the lost time. I really mean that.'

'Don't worry. Take your time,' he answered sarcastically. 'I wouldn't want to put you out.'

CHAPTER FIVE

ALIX drove at an almost reckless speed. Hidden by large sunglasses, her eyes were careful and she was fully aware of the fact that this was wildlife terrain. The Land Rover shook and bounced chaotically over the rutted track.

'Do you have to go so fast, Alix? Unless I'm reading the signs incorrectly, you're taking your temper out on the Land Rover.' Reed's voice contained anger.

Her quick glance was one of smouldering frustration.

'No, I don't *have* to go so fast.'

'Then why are you? Apart from landing us upside down, or in a ditch, you might hit some animal...'

'I won't,' she retorted. 'Don't worry.'

'How the hell do you know you won't?' He was completely losing patience with her.

'My eyes are trained. Why? Are you nervous?' She turned to look at him.

'Don't be sarcastic! You're acting like an irresponsible schoolgirl!'

Seething, Alix immediately slackened speed.

'Maybe you'd like to get out and hitch a lift—if you can get one?'

'Cut it out, Alix! How long is this to go on?'

'If you provoke me, what else can you expect? I've apologised. What more do you want?' Her nerves were strained to the point when she felt like shrieking.

Eventually, of course, the excitement of spotting wildlife took care of the rest of the day. Hugo and Mercedes were, as always, indefatigable spotters, and even Alix, in her present mood, was caught up in the excitement.

A swimming-pool glittered beneath the sun, and as Alix parked the Land Rover at the Marula Lodge, which was always hired as a complete unit, she said, 'Exclusively yours, Reed. I hope you and your friends enjoy your stay in Look-Out Safaris' private camp—Marula.'

'I intend to enjoy my stay here, Alix, and I believe that goes for everybody else. If you take my advice, you'll do the same, especially as you've mentioned that this is your first stay here.'

'I'm anything but a guest.' Her voice was brittle. 'That's stretching it a bit far. People who visit this camp, you see, either hire a Land Rover or come in their own Land Rover, which means the services of a guide are never necessary. We have three men here, by the way, who will cook the food we've brought, and they'll also do the general chores. I might just mention that they're of the Tawana tribe, but they can speak a little English.'

'While I appreciate the information, Alix, I'm inclined to be irritated by your tone. There's no need to get back on your high horse now that we've ar-

rived here.' Reed's impatience was coming to the
surface again.

Alix turned to open her door and then watched
moodily as Reed, who had lost no time in getting
out of the Land Rover, began to involve himself in
the offloading of the luggage. Apart from personal
luggage there were cartons of food, which had been
purchased in Maun. Meat, chicken and sausages
filled the built-in deep freeze, while other items were
stored in the compact refrigerator which was also
built into the custom-designed Land Rover.

During lunch, Alix found herself wondering
whether it would be wise to explain about Gerald,
but one look at Reed's hard profile warned her to
say nothing more about it.

At one stage, when she found herself alone with
him, he said, 'This position you have obviously in-
terferes with your private life. I wonder you carry
on with it.'

'My position of a game-viewing guide makes very
little difference to my private life, which is very
disciplined, as it happens.' Alix realised he was
goading her. 'Look, Reed, I know you're annoyed
with me. You don't understand anything about last
night, though.'

'That's where you're wrong. I understand perfectly. What's so unusual, after all, about intimacy
between consenting adults? But what I do *not*
understand is why you allowed *last night* to in-
terfere with your obligation towards this safari. You
were, I understand, supposed to have been on time

this morning.' His dark blue eyes were slowly beginning to blaze.

After a moment she said, 'You have me at a disadvantage there, and what's more, you're enjoying it. Nothing, it would appear, will make up for the fact that I shared my chalet with Gerald last night, and that I slept in this morning. What is it with you?'

'Maybe I'm jealous,' Reed answered curtly. 'This could be one of the side-effects of falling in love with my glamorously beautiful guide.'

'Ah, last night obviously bothers you, Reed. What you're actually *trying* to say is that you too would like to sleep with me! Why restrict that to Gerald?' Alix gave him a furious look as she got up and went to her chalet.

Some time later she heard him call her name. 'Alix?'

She went to the door, which was open, and stood regarding him with frustrated eyes. 'What is it you want? This is a total joke, Reed. I've never had ill-feeling with tourists on a safari before. I've been sitting here thinking about it, actually. Suddenly you come along—you and Camille—and you've both turned my work into a farce!'

'No, Alix.' His eyes went on holding hers.

'Yes, Reed.'

'Forget about Camille,' he went on. 'Treat her as you would a bitchy little thirteen-year-old—she certainly acts like one. I'm talking about us. We're here to get to know one another—to enjoy ourselves.'

'No, Reed, I don't have to enjoy myself. You and
your friends, on the other hand, are here to do just
that. You and Camille have come all the way from
France. Mercedes and Hugo have come from La
Réunion. You personally, I understand, have paid
a lot of money to enjoy this particular safari, but
that doesn't mean that your so-called glamorously
beautiful guide, who finds herself in the rather ridiculous position of having to share this private camp
with you, should join you for drinks beside the glittering pool—unless she drinks her own, which she
might just have brought along. What it amounts
to, very simply, is this. You've paid for my services,
along with the hire of the Land Rover. You've paid
for your accommodation and the accommodation
of your party. I'm here to drive you around so that
you can see, and learn, I hope, as much about animals as possible, and up to now, I'm sure you've
had no cause for complaint.'

'Don't be haughty with me, Alix. If I've arranged this safari and if I've paid a lot of money
for it, and if I happened to arrange with Look-Out
Safaris to have Alix Sandton as our guide—you
know as well as I do *why*. I wanted to see you again.'

'And yet you brought Camille along...'

'I gave Armand my word that I'd look after her.'

'Oh, for sure. I wonder if he'll ever find out just
how well you *did* look after her!'

'You're barking up the wrong tree. She's a spoilt
brat, but she is, in fact, a consenting adult. This
has *not* happened with me, so will you make a note
of that? It didn't happen on the first safari and it

hasn't happened on this one. I'm just not interested in going to bed with Miss Camille Boyer.'

'Anyway, you don't have to explain anything,' said Alix, trying not to show that she was relieved to hear this.

'I'm not explaining it. I'm merely telling you, Alix, since it seems to be bothering you. What do you take me for? Do you think I take every kid who throws herself at me to bed?' His eyes were blazing and Alix realised that she had gone too far, but it was useless to apologise.

'Is that all?' she asked stiffly.

'No, it's not all. I'll expect you at the pool in ten minutes. I want this and I believe you want it too. We'll take it from there.' Reed stretched out his hand and took her fingers between his own.

After a moment's reflection she said, very quietly, 'Very well.'

Like a miracle, peace existed during the following two days, and then, on the third day, Milton Ross arrived at the crack of dawn from the Sycamore Safari Lodge, to take the party to the Koenigs' private crocodile farm for the day. They were to return after dinner and viewing game, at night, was to be a highlight.

Alix believed she was to spend the day on her own at the Marula camp and almost looked forward to a restful period of swimming, lazing in the sun, reading maybe—but most of all, she intended to use this time to try and sort out her feelings towards Reed Forsythe.

What she had not been prepared for was the fact that Reed had planned to remain behind.

After Milton had driven off she turned to Reed. 'I thought you were going with them? I don't understand...'

'I had no intention of going. Do you think I'd leave you here alone?' he answered.

'Well, of course I thought that!' Looking at him, she thought, this man's bad news. He promises nothing but catastrophe in my life. She felt a rising panic.

'I'm not interested in crocodile farms, for God's sake, Alix! I've seen enough carpets of crocodiles on the last safari with Hugo, Mercedes, Jacques and Jacquetta to last me a lifetime. Armand is welcome to his venture.'

'You might have told me from the beginning, when you and Karl arranged this with Milton Ross, from Gaberone. In fact, Karl might have told me, for that matter.' Alix found herself thinking how Camille had accepted, with the usual bad grace, that Reed and Alix were to remain behind.

At that moment, while they were standing talking in front of the main building of the camp, one of the game guards came to tell them that breakfast had now been prepared for them, since the others had eaten before leaving for the crocodile farm.

Although it was not the first meal Alix had eaten with Reed, she felt tense and ill at ease. As he helped himself to sausages and eggs, which were being kept warm beneath burners, he said, 'Well, we have peace, perfect peace on our hands, Alix.'

This can't be happening, she thought.

'The peace will depend on you,' she answered shortly.

'Are we going to drive out into the sun?' He lifted his dark lashes to look at her.

'That's what I'm here for, after all. To drive you out into the sun—and tomorrow's sun.' Alix picked up her glass of orange juice and sipped from it slowly.

'On the other hand, we could stay here and just absorb the sun—swim—sunbathe...'

'You're basically a very scheming person,' she answered. 'Look, I have no idea what's behind all this, Reed, but whatever it is, I don't intend taking too much of it. I suggest we go game-spotting as soon as possible.'

'You don't want to be alone with me, is that it?' She was aware of the change in his eyes.

'We're not alone, or had you overlooked the fact that there happen to be three members of Look-Out Safaris' staff here? But, to get back to business, I have to point out again that I was hired to drive you and your party about in the Chobe Reserve. I am a guide, after all, not somebody laid on for you by an escort agency.'

'Sarcasm usually marks the inability to cope. What are you afraid of, Alix?' drawled Reed.

'You!' she told him furiously. 'Perhaps I'm overreacting, but—something about you. You knew you wouldn't be going to the crocodile farm with the others, and yet you omitted to tell me—not only me, but the others, who were, quite frankly, surprised when you announced that you'd be remaining behind.'

'Why do you think I planned all this? I came back to make it with you, as they say. Besides,' Reed's smile was mocking, 'I spent three days at a crocodile farm when I was in Kenya for a spell. What's more, I was thankful to leave. I have no affection towards crocs.'

'Tell me, Reed, on that occasion in Kenya did you have a female guide? Did you manage to make it with her?' There was angry frustration in her eyes.

'No, believe it or not. I drove my own Land Cruiser. Permit me, Alix, to correct the misapprehension that I rely on women to drive me around or keep me amused.'

'Well, I *am* impressed. I'm devoutly impressed, actually.' She stood up and flung her paper serviette down on the table. 'I'll meet you at the Land Rover in ten minutes' time. I'll take you on a very nice, exciting game-viewing excursion. This area is seething with animals—lots of lion. Don't forget to bring your camera. You might even get to take something for Camille's gallery.'

The sun was climbing and it tinged the skeletal trees and bush with pink and then pure gold. As they got into the Land Rover Alix said, 'We're going to leave the river.' She turned to look at Reed. He looked more super every day, she thought, more tanned. His skin, his dark blue eyes, his new beard and moustache—all had the power to excite her.

'Let's just say that I'm reasonably satisfied at what you've suggested.' There was mockery in his eyes.

'Good.' She gave him an elaborate safari guide smile.

They had been driving for about twenty minutes and Reed had taken a number of photographs of giraffe, buffalo, zebra, antelope and other game. Although she was used to game-spotting, Alix mostly enjoyed doing the same thing over and over again, and such was the case now. Reed was full of boyish charm, and his excitement was infectious.

They had stopped so that he could get a photo of a spotted, sloping hyena before it loped into the dust-coated bush, and as he turned round in his seat to put his camera on the seat behind he said, 'One part of me wants to know the worst about— Gerald.'

'Well, he's fair. He's fragile and, I think you will agree, he's very handsome. You saw that for yourself. What is this? Confession time?' Alix asked crossly.

Their eyes met and hers remained riveted on his handsome bearded face, before going to rest on his mouth. His face was not just handsome, she found herself thinking, it was strong, with a jawline which, although delicately fashioned, was hard. He had a firm chin—stubborn, maybe. As she looked at him, she felt vulnerable. As she listened to him, a part of her did not trust him—but perhaps this was because of the seeds of doubt which Camille had planted.

When he put his arms about her and kissed her she stiffened and then pulled away.

'Reed, let's get this straight. A long time ago I made a promise to myself not to become involved with any man during one of my safaris. Quite apart from that, you obviously—er—shift around when it comes to women!'

'Camille's been busy, hasn't she?' Reed expelled an angry breath. 'It's a pity, Alix, that you haven't learned to trust me as you obviously trust Camille. What is it with you? Let's get this straight—I want you in my life as I've never wanted any woman.'

'Please take your arms away.' Alix moved restlessly in his embrace, and when he released her she stared out of the windscreen for a few moments, while he watched her. She turned.

'What are we talking about, Reed? The fact that you want to take me to bed? Do you expect me to be over the moon?'

'Oh, come on, Alix! What is this? You have a hell of an opinion of me!'

Her lovely eyes brooded on his mouth and then lifted to meet his gaze, and then his arms were about her again, their lips meeting hungrily.

'I want you so much, Alix.' Reed always had a way of saying her name as if he had personally invented it, just for her. She wanted to believe in him. 'I want you—every bit of you—so much.'

Don't become this man's substitute lover, a little voice cautioned her.

'No,' she said against his searching mouth. 'This is not for me. I have no intention of giving myself to a man who feels I'm just another body to fool around with, Reed.'

'Don't you understand? I love you.' He drew back to look at her.

'No, you don't love me. I know it might have seemed like it a few moments ago, but I haven't exactly been waiting for you to come along and hand out favours. To use an expression—I'm not up for grabs. I know all about you.' Alix started the engine.

When they got back to the Marula Safari Lodge she parked the Land Rover and switched off the engine. There was the sound of garden clippers and then, as though the arrival of the Land Rover had been a call for peace, the clipping noises stopped abruptly.

Without a word to Reed Alix went straight to her chalet, which was cool and welcoming, and lost no time in taking a shower.

Later on she went to sit next to the pool, and thoughts of a beautiful girl named Theresa kept crowding in on her, and she felt depressed. As she saw Reed making his way to the pool, she turned her back.

'Alix?'

She did not turn, and he came round to where he could see her face.

'You look unhappy,' he said. 'Don't.'

'If I look unhappy, it's because I *am* unhappy,' she retorted.

'Why?'

'Why? Oh, don't make me laugh, Reed! You're doing your best to get me into some wild, irrational affair without knowing what the future has to offer, and it would appear that there's nothing. Into the bargain, there's this girl—Theresa...'

'There was no point in telling you about her.' Reed's voice had an edge.

'And yet you wanted to know about Gerald,' she pointed out.

'Gerald turned up. Right?'

'Maybe Theresa will too. Then you wouldn't need me. You wouldn't need Camille.'

'Don't be childish, Alix!' snapped Reed.

'I can be very childish when the occasion arises. It just depends how you look at it. Maybe you've got the word wrong. Maybe you mean childlike. In other words, having the good qualities of a child, such as innocence, frankness. That's more to the point.'

'It's over with Theresa...'

'Oh, go to hell!' She hunched her shoulders.

With stunning effect, she was wearing a vineyard-green pareu over a black one-piece swimsuit which was deeply V'd back and front, with high-cut legs. Every time she moved, her long tanned legs came into view. Her earrings resembled gold tassels, but there the resemblance ended, for they were tough and she would not have to take them off if she decided to swim.

Reed reached for her wrists before she could stop him, and pulled her up beside him. 'Why are we going on like this, when all we want to do is to get to know and understand one another? I love you.'

She turned her head so that she would not have to look at him.

'Are you listening to any of this?' he asked angrily.

'No. My ears are closed.'

Placing his hands on either side of her head, he turned her face so that he could look into her eyes, and, weakening under the spell of his dark blue eyes, she was no longer ashamed of her feelings for him. Was it, perhaps, that she had made up her mind to live for the moment? Live for the moment, and handle her crash landing later.

'Do you know what Gerald said to me after you left?' he asked.

'I don't want to know. I don't want to talk about Gerald.'

'In any case, I'll tell you. He said—so I have a rival.'

'In other words, a competitor for some prize— the prize being me? Oh, come! Do you think I have no say in the matter? What did you say, pray?' Alix had decided to climb back on her high horse.

'I said, may the best man win. What else?'

His remark began immediately to nag her. She moved away from him. 'You're both far too ambitious. Do you think I might have a shandy?'

'Of course. You can have champagne if you like.'

'Right now, a shandy would be perfect,' she told him.

As they sat over their drinks she studied him when he wasn't looking. She wondered how she could bring the conversation back to Theresa again.

There was the usual easy grace about Reed as he put his glass down and went to dive into the water. He swam, she saw, like everything else he did—strongly and with a good style. His strokes propelled him swiftly through the water, and in no time he was at the other side of the pool. Flipping over beneath the water, he swam to where Alix's chair was placed nearby.

'Come on.' He held out a dripping tanned hand.

'Later.' Laughing a little, Alix sat back and crossed her legs, and she saw his eyes go to her toes which, like her fingernails, were beautifully lacquered. Her slim body remained motionless and elegant, but the fingers of one hand stroked the gold bracelet which gleamed in the sun. Without realising it, she appeared effortlessly beautiful, smooth and cool—a girl who worked competently and serenely through the day to make game-viewing a success until the time came when she could sit back and enjoy a tall glass containing shandy, or the juice of some exotic fruit.

'The water is very invigorating. Feel my hand,' Reed invited, but she refused to touch him.

'I'll take your word for it.'

He hoisted himself out of the water and, reaching for her hand, he pulled her up beside him and rested his cool forehead against her dry, sun-warmed skin.

'You're wetting me,' she said, laughing.

This time, when he put his arms around her, she did not protest, and she felt the shock waves beginning to swamp her. Every nerve in her body was aroused. She thought, why not? I want him, just as he wants me.

'In Zimbabwe, the ruins, Victoria Falls and,' Reed laughed softly, and nuzzled her ear, 'even at yet another damned crocodile farm, I thought of you all the time. I came back to see why. At first, I'll admit I had designs on making love to you and—take it from there. But things took on a complete new meaning for me. The desire to possess you, Alix Sandton, soon developed into something more, where I felt I wanted you in my life—*permanently*. Now I know why I came back.'

Alix still didn't know what to thin! so she kept quiet.

'You don't believe me, do you?' Reed's eyes searched hers.

'No. You're a mystery to me.'

'I love you. Remember that when I'm kissing you, Alix.'

'Don't you really mean—remember that when what I *really* have in mind, Alix, is to get you into bed with me before I clear off back to France?'

'You have a very distorted image of me.' His blue eyes narrowed.

She had put her glass down on the grass and, breaking away from him, she picked it up and walked over to a low, sun-warmed wall and leaned one slim hip against it. She took a sip of her drink, then said, 'Reed, you know I'm going through a conflict right now, don't you?'

'Yes.' His eyes went over her. 'I do know. Exactly *why*, though, beats me. Is it because of Gerald? Was marriage on the agenda?'

'I notice you say *was*. You're very sure of that, aren't you? Marriage with Gerald has never formed part of my plans, as it happens. For that matter, marriage has never been top of Gerald's priority list. Do you think he wants to feel tied down? But to get back to the present time—in other words, *us*. God knows, I'm tempted. You know that, of course, and that's why you keep going to work on me.'

The game warden interrupted them. 'Lunch is ready,' he told them.

Lunch consisted of perfectly chilled, perfectly sliced tinned ham, potato salad, cheese and fruit, and they had it next to the pool. Reed poured wine. They did not speak much, but Alix was aware that he was watching her carefully.

Afterwards he lay face downwards in the sun, while she sat in a chair. She was wearing nothing else now but her black, deeply slashed swimsuit and a floppy straw magenta-pink hat which packed beautifully into her case.

Reed turned over and raised himself so that he could give her a long look.

'What are you so deep in thought about?' he asked eventually, just when Alix thought her heart was going to stop.

'I've decided to. What else? At least, when we make love, you're not married. Or are you? I'm not even sure, if it comes to that! I mean—who *is* Theresa?' She spread her hands.

'Oh, for God's sake, Alix!' Reed was furious now, and he took a long calming breath.

'By the way,' Alix went on, because she couldn't help herself, 'what is she like? Beautiful? Sophisticated? Rich, like you?'

'Forget about her! It's over!' Reed erupted like a bolt of lightning.

'Oh, sure. They're all over, very conveniently. In any case, what does it matter? I've decided to be just another name on the list...'

'I see you have a venomous tongue when it suits you.' He started to walk away, then stopped. 'I'm going to my chalet for a towel. Is there anything you want?'

'A nice big box of chocolates.'

'Be serious, Alix,' he snapped.

When he returned she was in the pool. He had changed into trousers and a white T-shirt and he looked very tanned.

'I'm sorry,' she said, looking up at him. 'I'm giving you a bad time, aren't I?'

'No. I'm enjoying every moment,' he answered sarcastically.

As she got out of the pool she said, 'I'm going to wash my hair. Maybe a little later we could walk to the look-out and watch the animals as they come to the river to drink?'

'That will be fine.'

'What time will the others be back?' she asked, a little too casually. 'Have you any idea?'

'Milton said about ten-thirty.'

Their eyes met briefly, before she left him to go to her chalet.

CHAPTER SIX

ALIX'S eyes went straight to the bottle of champagne, which she knew Reed had purchased in Maun, and the two glasses held carelessly between the fingers of one hand.

'Being organised is important,' he said.

'Oh, I agree.' Her eyes condemned him. Somehow his remark nagged her.

He watched her as she came down the shallow steps of her chalet.

'I'll carry your binoculars and camera, if you like.' She held out her hand.

'I can manage, but you can take the binoculars. You might want to use them on the way to the look-out.' Neatly bearded and moustached, he reminded her of a tanned, handsome and unscrupulous adventurer. They always do, these types, she thought as something seemed to twist her heart.

Molten-pink bougainvillaea cascaded over a white pillar beside the gate, which was open and led up to the look-out, which was on a higher level than the chalets. Behind them the sun, still strong, sun-dazzled the whiteness of the chalets and main building and highlighted the golden thatched roofs.

The look-out was built in the form of a small amphitheatre with curved cement ledges to act as seating. The whole structure hugged the contours of the half-moon shape of the rocky hill. Down below, the banks of the river were green with trees and vegetation which gave way to a vast plain of dried grass and scrubby bush.

Reed put the champagne and the glasses in a shady spot, while Alix watched him with a thrill of excitement as she tried to recapture a feeling of lightheartedness.

'It's going to be marvellous in a little while,' she said. 'There's going to be a dramatic sunset, I think. Already some animals are on their way to the banks of the river to drink. And to think, we have this all to ourselves!'

For a while, tension was forgotten while they took turns in sharing the binoculars, then Alix went to stand at the wooden railings.

There was a silence between them, then Reed said, 'What about some champagne?'

She turned to look at him. 'I'm so pleased you brought it. I'd love some.' Suddenly she meant it, and she went on watching him as he began to ease the cork from the bottle. Her eyes went to his watch—a Concord, with gold enhancing the natural stainless steel which gleamed at his wrist, and for no particular reason she immediately thought of Theresa, in France, and felt let down and was having second thoughts about letting Reed make love to her.

Looking away, she rested her head against one of the poles which supported the thatched roof. Behind her she heard the loud pop of the cork as it exploded and took off into the bush.

'Don't ask me to rescue that cork,' she said. 'I don't want to get eaten alive. There's always the possibility of a lurking wild animal, and there's always that element of danger to these camps.'

'Excitement, and an element of danger, seem to appeal to you,' Reed commented.

Alix was silent for a moment, then she said, 'Tell me, though, what was the champagne really supposed to be in aid of, when you set off from Maun? Had you visualised another conquest?' As she spoke, jealousy and hurt spilled into her eyes. 'Or aren't I supposed to ask?'

He came over to where she was standing.

'What's all this in aid of?' His voice was hard and demanded an answer.

'I'm in love with you, and I'm confused,' she answered in a small voice.

He had left the frothing glasses on the ledge to put his hands on her shoulders and turn her round so that he could look into her eyes.

'What are you confused about?' he asked.

'You.'

His arms closed about her and he held her close, and she seemed to fit perfectly to his masculine body.

'I love you. Don't be confused about this,' he told her.

Yes, but enough for what? her nerves shrieked. Marriage? Going back to France with you—with or without marriage? *What?*

When he kissed her, and went on kissing her, it was as if she had once again let the atmosphere of

Marula charm her into accepting what was happening between them. She was also aware of the tightrope on which she was walking and beginning to lose her balance, for she realised that she had accepted the inevitable of having Reed make love to her and every moment was bringing that moment closer.

When she could get her breath she said, 'What about the champagne? It'll be going flat.' She laughed a little as she broke away from him. 'Oh look, Reed—elephants down at the river! Isn't it wonderful? This sort of thing never fails to thrill me. I always feel privileged and exhilarated.'

The sun was gilding everything. Reed went for the champagne and a moment later he was passing her a glass. It was almost like being on honeymoon, Alix found herself thinking, as they sipped the champagne and gazed down at the river. Zebra and buck had also arrived at the water's edge.

Reed refilled their glasses and she said, 'Let's drink this on the way back to the chalets. The sun is just about to fall into the bush, away from sight. It'll be dark soon.'

On the way she stopped negotiating the steps and, giggling a little, she said, 'I feel wonderfully disorientated. It must be the fresh air.'

Reed came closer so that he could kiss her and she felt like drowning in her helpless desire for him. 'I'll spill my champagne.' She held her glass so that he would not bump it.

When they reached her chalet he took her glass away from her and put it down along with his own and the empty bottle, on the low wall, then he took her into his arms and they stood swaying together, their bodies arching and straining to get closer.

From the beginning, Alix was thinking, she'd had no intention of losing control, and yet here she was almost giving herself to him and surprising herself as much as she was surprising him, no doubt. She knew she was totally in love with him, and she was going to allow him to make love to her in the full knowledge that, for her, there could be possible heartache, for what did she really know about Reed Forsythe? Camille had painted a picture, and the picture wasn't pretty. Reed was a playboy.

'I want to love you properly,' he was saying, as he went on kissing her. 'Let me, Alix...'

He released her to open the screen door and when they were inside she said, almost flippantly in her nervousness, 'I'm not as wise as some of your women. You'll have to—to...'

'For God's sake, don't talk like that! You talk as though there've been... what do you take me for? Some kind of depraved sex maniac?'

In a quiet voice Alix said, 'What you don't understand is that I've accepted that I'm about to become a...'

'A what?' Reed cut in. 'Go on, tell me!'

'I've been cautious, up to now. I haven't been made love to before. I'm totally—well, let's change that to—I'm relatively inexperienced.'

'Forget it, Alix! It's OK.'

'No, it's not OK,' she insisted. 'I *want* you to love me. I'm just—warning you. I know it sounds like a big deal. Well, it *is* a big deal to me.'

He came back to her and took her into his arms and buried his lips in her hair. They seemed to be drowning in each other's needs. Alix tried not to be too conscious about the expert way in which he undressed her—as he had undressed Theresa and countless other women. His share of casual affairs? Why am I so jealous? she asked herself. Why am I taking this so seriously? This is the age of the permissive society. People have become liberal in sexual matters.

She found herself saying, 'Just be patient with me.'

Reed stopped kissing her, but only so that he could pick her up and carry her to one of the beds in the room. A moment later he had joined her and, shyly, she began to unbutton his shirt and undo his belt. He left her side so that he could shed the rest of his clothing, then, as he gathered her into his arms again, they looked at each other in shared desire.

Although her longing was as great as his, Alix managed to hang on to some sanity, for she was not yet free of sexual scruples. 'You're helping me to make such a mess of my life,' she murmured. She didn't think he'd heard, but he had, and his response was to draw back from her immediately. His face, she saw, had gone cold and he rolled away from her and lay on his stomach, breathing hard, and she knew he was fighting for control.

She struggled to fight her own way out of desire, and after a while she said, 'Reed, I'm sorry. It's just that I don't know what to make of you.'

He did not answer for a moment, then he said, 'OK. You're out of the danger zone, Alix. There'll be no havoc in your life. You either know what to make of me by now, or you don't.'

He swung his legs over the side of the bed and grabbed his shirt, which he had flung on the other bed. She watched him as he shrugged himself into the sleeves. He did not bother to do up the buttons of the shirt and, feeling sheer despair, Alix closed her eyes, and when she opened them again he had his back to her and was zipping up his white canvas trousers.

He turned. 'I find I have no wish to take advantage of you, Alix.'

'I told you—it—was—OK.' She put her fingertips to her cheeks. 'Anyway, since when have you become so sensitive?' She wanted to hurt him back. 'Look, Camille will be arriving back soon, and you know how jealous *she* is. You'd better go.'

'If I were you, lady, I'd shut my ears to what Camille has to say.' Reed's eyes were blazing.

'I don't want a speech from you!' shouted Alix. 'Just get out of here!'

'I intend to, don't worry!' he shouted back.

Some time later there was a light knock on her door. The game guard had come to explain that he had prepared the meal and Alix realised that they had not had dinner. For appearances' sake, she said, 'Thank you. I'll be there shortly.' She felt totally inadequate and despairing.

There was really nothing else for it, she thought as she crossed the lawn a little later. She was wearing jeans and a low-cut pink shirt, which had just happened to be at the top of her holdall when she was searching for something to wear.

Reed was busy turning the meat on the barbecue and without looking at her he said, 'Come and tell me what you want, Alix.'

'Anything—I'm not fussy.'

'Bring a plate.' His voice was curt, giving nothing away.

'After what's happened, I'd rather not be here,' she told him.

He swung round. 'What's happened, Alix, is— quite simply, I've come to my senses.'

A little later, and without her permission, he filled her glass with wine.

'I didn't *want* wine,' she said crossly.

'Why not?' he snapped.

'I'm in no mood to celebrate, that's why.'

'I'm not asking you to celebrate. On the contrary.' He spoke with considerable impatience. 'Frankly, Alix, I'm finding all this excessive. Just eat, drink and shut up, will you?'

'In other words, I mustn't make too much of it?'

'Forget it. That's all it amounts to, damn it.'

'Oh, sure. Anyway, what does it matter, Reed? I came to my senses—you came to yours.'

'Maybe it was the other way round? Huh?' he answered sarcastically.

An animal screamed in the night and Alix thought, join the club, pal. I feel like screaming myself.

In her bewildered fury she wanted to lash out at him.

'From what I can make out, your first consideration has always been yourself!'

When she got up and left him Reed made no attempt to call her back or to follow her. Some time later she heard Milton Ross's open Land Rover arriving back, and she felt overwhelmingly depressed.

Her light was still burning when Reed knocked on her door. Wearing a black silk kimono which was adrift with sprays of dark pink impala lilies, she hesitated for a moment before she went to open it. 'What is it?' she asked curtly.

'You'll have gathered that the others are back,' said Reed.

'I'm about to get into bed. Is that all you came to tell me?'

'No, it's not all I came to tell you.'

'Well, I have no desire to talk to you, Reed.'

'I'm concerned about you,' he told her. 'God, you're stubborn, Alix!'

'You're *concerned* about me? I have difficulty in believing that. Camille...'

He cut in angrily, 'Don't bring Camille into this. I'm usually misquoted by Camille. Only you can choose to go on believing the worst of me, or you can choose to trust me. It's entirely up to you.' He came into her room. 'So, what's it to be?'

'I've been lying on my bed feeling sorry for myself.' Alix took a breath and then released it loudly. 'I thought about what happened earlier this evening and I wondered how I could have contemplated adding myself to that list.'

'What list are you talking about? Let me tell you something, the list is not as long as you believe it to be. There was not one name to build my life around. Up to the present time, no other woman has mattered to me. You've grown to mean more to me than any woman I've ever known.' Reed took her into his arms and kissed her, and she clung to him.

'I love you,' she said. 'I *do* . . .'

Later, when they were in bed, he was slow and tender with her. She realised that he wanted to be gentle and that he was exercising extreme control over his own desires. She was innocent and trusting and Reed was experienced—what did it matter?— and very tender.

'Darling,' he said, before they slept, 'you're going to have to learn French. You realise that, don't you?'

'I refuse to worry about that now,' Alix laughed softly as she nestled into him.

They came awake at the same moment, and Reed rolled over and reached for her immediately. This time she enjoyed a feeling of aggression which allowed her to make certain advances—the kind of advances which would have shocked her the first time he'd made love to her.

It was dawn when he left her, and Alix realised that in a few minutes the sun would be heaving itself out of the bush and then proceed to fill the whole terrain with a magical red glow.

Reed looked wonderful, she thought later, as he walked towards the Land Rover where she stood waiting.

'Your guide awaits you,' she said, smiling.

'I love you,' he said, very softly. 'What's more, there's a wonderful glow about you this morning.'

'It's the sun.' She went on smiling.

'It's not just the sun and you know it,' he teased. 'We'll come back here one day, just you and I. What do you say?'

'I'd love that—and no crocodile farms!' She laughed lightly—then stiffened as Camille, followed by Hugo and Mercedes, came towards them.

They arrived back at the Sycamore Safari Lodge in the afternoon, having stopped for lunch at an authorised picnic spot. Luggage was sorted out and taken to the right chalets.

When they were alone Reed said, 'You look tired, darling. It was a long haul back to the Lodge.'

'I confess to feeling a little stiff.' Alix smiled, then bit her lip. Their eyes met.

'Next time we do a safari, I'll drive,' he said.

'Oh, come! I'm not complaining. Don't tell me you believe that human abilities are determined by whether one happens to be male or female.' Her eyes were full of mockery.

'After you've settled in, we'll have a sundowner. I think we have another bottle of champagne in the refrigerator.' He reached for her hand and kissed her fingertips. 'We've got something to celebrate.'

A few moments later Alix saw him from her window, as he strode in the direction of the main building. He was probably going to attend to money matters, she thought; change for tipping, since they were leaving early in the morning.

Reed was nowhere to be seen when she went along to his patio, and after waiting for a while, she decided to go back to her own chalet and watch for him as he returned from Reception.

She was sitting on her own patio, feeling decidedly restless and let down, when Camille called out, 'You have been discarded, Alix?'

Alix felt her temper rising. 'Why? Do I *look* discarded?'

Camille laughed, her dark hair ruffled by the breeze which had suddenly got up. 'Yes, you do, actually.'

Alix watched her moodily as she made her way towards the main building—to look for Reed, no doubt. Acting on an impulse, she got up and decided to go for a walk in the direction of the terrace, where she met Werner Olivier, a guide for Early Bird Safaris.

'Hi there.' He sounded pleased to see her. 'Where are you heading for?'

'Nowhere in particular. Hi. How are you? The river looks wonderful, doesn't it?'

'What about having a drink with me?' he asked.

'Well, actually, I . . .' Alix turned away, her eyes searching for Reed. 'I was just on the verge of turning back.'

'I'm going to get myself a beer. Let me bring you something,' said Werner.

'I was going to have a drink with—er—one of my passengers, but I seem to have lost him.' She tried to sound carefree, but she was seething. Reed had been gone an age.

'It will do him good to look for you,' Werner answered cheerfully. 'Wait here, Alix. I'll be back.'

What is this? she thought, a little angrily. Why should I stand around waiting for these guys? I'm leaving—but Werner was already on his way back with the drinks.

'Let's sit over here.' He led the way to a garden bench. 'It does a person good to get away from the group now and again. In my case, a bunch of glamorous widows, average age forty-two to fifty.' He let out an impatient breath. 'Half the time they see nothing. They're too busy talking to spot any game.' He passed Alix a shandy, which he had mixed for her. 'Cheers.'

'Cheers, Werner. I'm going to be very rude, I'm virtually going to gulp this down and then leave you.'

While she sipped her shandy he talked about his work in general and asked her questions about Look-Out Safaris.

Glancing at her watch, an hour later, Alix said, 'Goodness, look at the time! I must be going. Thanks for the shandy, Werner—and the chat. Keep smiling. Maybe the next safari will consist of a bunch of glamorous models—average twenty-two to thirty-two. I'll hold thumbs for you.'

'It's been great, Alix.' He stood up. 'I'll be making my way back presently.'

She was passing Camille's chalet when Camille called out, 'Just a moment, Alix—I have something to give you. Reed asked me to give you this envelope.'

As Alix took the envelope she said. 'But I don't get this—where *is* Reed?'

'Prepare for a shock, Alix. Reed has left the Sycamore on the first stage to France. However, the other arrangements remain the same. You will drive us to the airstrip tomorrow...'

Feeling quite bewildered, Alix cut in, 'Is this some kind of joke?'

'Why should I joke about such matters? What else did you expect of Reed, Alix?'

'You make it sound so easy. Reed has left on the *first stage to France*—just like that! We happen to be in a game reserve. We're not anywhere near some international airport.' Alix glanced at the envelope, on which was printed, very simply, Alix.

'Reed left in a hurry,' Camille went on. 'He availed himself of an offer of a seat on a private Cessna Stationaire, which was due to leave almost immediately.'

'Why did he go?' Alix spoke with difficulty. 'I mean—this is just beyond me. We don't have take-offs every three minutes in the Chobe.'

'And yet the man with whom you have an involvement arrived during our last stay here at the safari lodge and then left the following morning, did he not? Private planes come and go, I should imagine.' Camille lifted one shoulder. 'I am not here to answer questions. I warned you of this, did I not?'

Suddenly she started to cry, and Alix stared at her, speechless.

'Reed has gone to Theresa, Alix. I have wanted Reed for so long. I have always hated Theresa. To go away with Reed on this safari seemed too wonderful to be true—and then *you* came along!'

Alix was experiencing her first real insight into Camille's nature and the problems which played havoc with her emotions.

'But it's supposed to be all over between Reed and—Theresa,' she said, with angry helplessness.

'*Huh!*' Camille drew a shuddering breath. 'You saw for yourself the photograph taken at the château. Did it look as if it was "all over", as you refer to it? You can see how *I* have suffered, Alix.'

'Yes, I can,' Alix replied, as if she were addressing a child. 'Well, you know what they say— there are plenty more pebbles on the beach, Camille.'

With shaking fingers, in the privacy of her own chalet, Alix opened the envelope, expecting to see a note, or even a letter, of explanation. Instead, the envelope contained two very substantial banknotes. A closer inspection revealed that there was no letter.

Pale, composed and furious, she went along to Reed's chalet. His belongings were gone. Except for a magazine and an almost empty bottle of expensive shampoo in the waste-paper basket, there was nothing. All that had been left behind was a nice fat tip for the very accommodating safari guide, for services rendered...while *on* safari.

Her first reaction was to tear the money up and send the pieces back to him, for she knew she would be able to get his address from Karl, but on second thoughts she put the money in her bag, where it would remain to remind her of female degradation and to think twice before giving herself to another man. When she had done that, she began to pack for the morning. She knew that if she were honest with herself, she had drawn out the interlude with Werner in an attempt to show Reed that she was not prepared to sit around waiting on him to get back from Reception just when it suited him.

Well, she had gone into her affair with her eyes wide open. Already she was regretting it. Her humiliation accounted for that.

To save face, she sat with Werner Olivier at dinner, and she was determined not to show her distress and her humiliation by making enquiries at Reception as to why Reed had left.

Camille refused to let the matter drop, and the next morning she said, 'Reed thinks only of himself. He has made a lot of money, and money, as everyone knows, has its uses. Women fall over him.

You will have to forget him, Alix. He has gone back
to his wife. He could not get away quick enough,
once he saw how serious you had become. The arrival of the Cessna was like a godsend to him.'

'Don't go to extremes, Camille. I know the whole
story—Reed told me about Theresa. You're not
telling me anything new. Theresa is not Reed's wife.'

'So that is what he told you? Theresa is Reed's
wife. Believe me—I should know. This girl has
caused me unbelievable jealousy. I was in love,
secretly, with Reed long before Theresa came into
his life, and I have gone on loving him.'

Directly Alix got back to Look-Out Safaris in
Gaberone, Karl Sievewright said, 'What are you
looking so put out about?'

'I don't think I look put out,' she answered.

'You want to take a look in the mirror.' His eyes
went over her.

'A report will have to go to Maun about the Land
Rover,' she told him. 'I was no sooner on the way
when I discovered I had a slow leak in one of the
tyres. I mean, why aren't these things checked
properly?'

They discussed this for a few moments, then Karl
said, 'So you had problems on this safari, did you?'

'Well, yes, I did.' Alix was thinking she still had
to give Maggie a piece of her mind for supplying
Gerald with information about her whereabouts in
the Chobe and the fact that this had led to embar-
rassment and unpleasantness.

On an impulse she said, 'By the way, Karl, if any letters arrive for me from Reed Forsythe, will you have them returned to France for me?'

'What's the big problem?' he asked.

'He happens to be married, that's the big problem.' Her voice was brittle. 'He might write, and then, on the other hand, he might not.'

'You had trouble with this guy last time, didn't you?'

'I had trouble with his girlfriend—one of his girlfriends.' Alix realised she was being childish and wished she'd had the good sense to keep her mouth shut.

'If a letter, or letters, arrive take my tip and tear them up and return the bits yourself,' advised Karl. 'Why don't you just do that?'

'I'm afraid I might just weaken and read what he has to say. I don't want Maggie handling this, otherwise I wouldn't have asked you.'

'Why don't you just ignore them?' Karl was rubbing his chin with his thumb. 'You women...talk about Women's Lib! You've got a lot to learn.'

'I wanted to insult him,' she retorted, inflamed. 'I'm sorry I asked you. Just—tear them up and put them in the waste-paper basket. Besides, I don't even know if he *will* write.'

'I'll handle it for you. So you've made a fool of yourself?' His eyes were thoughtful, and he drew the words out unfeelingly. 'Well, just see to it that you don't get so involved next time. How else do you expect these flings to end?'

Alix did not explain that she intended submitting her resignation and that, apart from working her notice, there would be no—next time.

'I'll go to work on this guy if he does write,' Karl called after her, as she went to the door. 'Just you leave it to me.'

CHAPTER SEVEN

ENVELOPED in what she called her white Saudi robe, Alix opened her mail. She felt more relaxed after her bath. The water had been foamy and fragrant and it had half filled her apricot-hued marble bath.

There was a long letter from her mother and a postcript from her father which made her suddenly homesick for Zimbabwe with its mountains, waterfalls, pine forests and ancient ruins.

Instead of cheering her up, the letter left her feeling depressed, and she went through to the kitchen to plan what she would have for dinner. Whatever it was, it would come out of the deep freeze. She decided on a chicken and mushroom pie, and it would go into her microwave oven when she was ready.

A few minutes later she slipped on a cobalt blue Bengali cotton caftan, which was always super to relax in, and then, to prove that one did not have to have a man around to dress up for, she put on the golden beads from Nigeria and the bracelet to match. For good measure, she would dine by candlelight—the fragrant ones. Her wine was perfectly chilled and it would be sipped from one of the antique long-stemmed glasses which her mother had given her.

All alone, she thought, and began to hum the melody which had been popular in her mother's day—or was it her *grand*mother's? I'm all alone, So what? She felt pampered, even though she'd had to do all the pampering herself. She felt serene and in control of her life. 'Into the bargain,' she said aloud, 'I'm experienced. Reed Forsythe has seen to that, in brackets.' It felt good—or did it?

Look-Out Safaris were never short of tourists and she knew she would be back in the Chobe Game Reserve after a short break at home which would be spent attending to her clothes, cleaning the cottage and shopping.

During the following days she applied for any position which even remotely revolved around advertising.

Two more game-viewing safaris followed, and throughout each, Alix struggled to keep her mind off Reed, but everywhere she went she was reminded of him.

When she got home from the second safari there was a letter from a firm called Latest Concept, asking her to telephone for an appointment. She was a successful candidate and had to break the news to Karl, who threw a tantrum. To fit in her period of notice, she did one more safari, and then it was all over and her feelings were confused.

Gerald was back in her life—not that he had ever gone out of it, really. He responded to what he referred to as her sexually unresponsive nature with unconcealed hostility.

'I'm not going to see you any more,' Alix said one night, after she had welcomed and then rejected his advances at the last moment. 'I didn't want this to happen.' There was despair in her voice.

'Well, it didn't happen. What the hell!' The harshness in his voice upset her even more. '*As usual.* So what are you going on about?' They were in his penthouse, as he always liked to refer to it, after having been out to dine. 'What it amounts to is you're asking me to control myself, after you've succeeded in working me up. Right?'

'You're implying something I don't like, Gerald,' said Alix angrily. 'Sometimes you can be so callous!'

'Whether you happen to like it or not, it happens to be true.' She grieved to see the hurt and antagonism in his ice-blue eyes. Looking at him, she thought how easy it would be to give in and then go on giving in, first with Gerald and then, since Gerald had no intention of being serious, with someone else.

'Oh, spare me the tragic looks,' he was saying. 'Quite frankly, Alix, I've had enough of this stunted relationship.'

She gave him a long, considering look. 'Don't, Gerald. I'm not some tramp you've just picked up. Don't let's part this way.'

His lips curved sarcastically. 'Sometimes, Alix, I wish to hell you were a tramp.' He ran his finger round the rim of his glass and she was aware of the hard anger in his voice. 'What is it you want? A fancy gold band and a useless certificate? Is that so very important to you?'

She did not answer for a moment, then she said, 'Marriage happens to be the last thing on my mind.'

As he drove her home Gerald said, 'Well, I guess you might as well know it. I've met a lavish girl. She's made up for our impoverished relationship.'

Alix felt a spurt of temper. 'So I've been feeling guilty for nothing?'

'It's been uphill all the way with you,' he said. 'I reasoned, though, the ultimate goal was worth waiting for.' He still sounded bitter and outraged at her rejection of him.

'You've had success elsewhere, so what are you so worried about?' It was her turn to sound outraged now.

Well, that was that, she thought as she prepared for bed. She asked herself why she had just gone on drifting with Gerald.

Suddenly she felt a surge of elation. Her job and her cottage were all that mattered now, at this stage of her life.

Because of the diploma she held and her past experience in advertising, she had stepped into a top position. Her thoughts often went to the difficult time when she had to adjust from being a wildlife guide to being tied down to office hours and an office desk. *In an office!* In the end, though, she had settled down.

There was a new restless energy about her. Her L-shaped, ivory-lacquered desk was indicative of what lay ahead in the days, weeks and months to

come—an accumulation of work, internal memor-
anda, reports, letters and brochures. Latest
Concept, she'd soon discovered, was a new venture,
and this alone made her work an enormous challenge. She was impatient to leave the cottage in the
morning and reluctant to leave the office in the late
afternoon. She fully intended being instrumental in
making this business a huge success.

In between, she went to a number of very private
parties where interesting people stood around
talking. At other private disco parties she danced
to hot sultry music which she never permitted to
affect her in any way. In her need not to be swept
up into an affair she was often selfish, refusing a
second—or third or fourth—date, depending on
how dangerous she felt her companion to be if she
found him physically exciting. She swam in other
people's private pools and she became even more
tanned and glossy. Men told her how beautiful and
exciting she was . . . women, how lovely.

Once, when she was spring-cleaning the cottage,
she felt a king-sized shock when she came across
the money which Reed had so callously left for her,
and she was a lot less sure of her memories of him.

As her annual leave drew closer she realised that
if she wanted to get away, she would have to start
planning.

'What about Tuscany?' Tootie Seboko asked one
day, as they were having coffee in Alix's office.
'Look, Alix, at this wonderful villa.' She passed
Alix one of the brochures which Alix had been given
by a travel agency. 'Or what about an island? Look,

it says here—visit *our* lush green island, where the cares of *your* world will be easily forgotten. Listen to our sweeping casuarina trees sighing and to the pulsating beat of the sega by night. Live one of your wildest fantasies. Come to Mauritius.'

'I've been to Mauritius.' Alix bit into a wafer biscuit.

'Well, what about Madagascar or the Seychelles?' Tootie went on, her long dark fingers, tipped by lengthy red nails, fluttering through the various brochures on Alix's desk.

'What about La Réunion?' Alix's voice sounded taut, even to her own ears. 'There's a man there who owns a number of chalets. I've always remembered his name, Armand Leclerc.'

'Where did you meet this man?' Tootie laughed gaily. 'This man is a skeleton in the cupboard, perhaps?'

'You could refer to him as a skeleton in the cupboard, when I come to think of it. I'd have to find out his full address from the agency. The chalets must be listed.' Alix lifted her telephone and began to dial the number of a travel agency.

The chalets *were* listed, and she wrote direct to Armand Leclerc.

She thought she would never hear, and then a letter arrived from the island in the Indian Ocean in which she was advised that yes, indeed, such a chalet—suitable for one person—did exist, and her instructions were awaited. In turn, she lost no time in writing back and reserving the accommodation, then she booked a seat on a plane and organised her travellers' cheques. After she had done all this, she had the sensation of intense excitement.

Moving competently through the days before her holiday, she cleared the demanding piles of paper on her desk until, satisfied, she sat back in her ivory swivel chair and took a long, deep breath.

Because of an electrical problem, and after a three-hour delay, the plane to La Réunion was of course late. Eventually the passengers were permitted to cross the tarmac towards the stairs which led up to the big curved door, where flight attendants stood smiling at the entrance and revealing nothing of the tiredness caused by hours of waiting about.

The plane taxied to the runway, and after waiting for clearance to take off, it began to move, then gathered speed and hurtled along until the nose lifted. By this time Alix's nerves were at jangling point and she closed her eyes and listened to the landing gear shaking itself free of the tarmac.

Soon after the passengers had been welcomed aboard and briefed on seat-belts, oxygen and other information, the seat-belt lights dimmed and went off, and over the address system, the Captain's smooth voice expressed regret at the inconvenience caused to passengers. He hoped, nevertheless, that they would enjoy the flight.

Glamorous stewardesses began serving drinks and Alix was handed hers, which she felt she needed. Although she had often flown, she had never felt as strung up and nervous as she did now, especially as there was turbulence. Was it because she was

going to La Réunion, she wondered, where there
was a remote—but possible, just possible, chance
that she would come face to face with Reed
Forsythe?

Later, dinner was served, and she sipped her wine
and, as always, looked sleek, sophisticated and
beautiful.

Since she had not booked through a travel agency
she began to worry, as there would be no one to
meet her at the airport and, instead of landing in
daylight, she would be landing at night and on an
island where French was the order of the day.

At long last the chimes came on and the voice
of a stewardess instructed that passengers should
put their seats in an upright position and adjust
their seat-belts for landing. The seats of the plane
began to slope and after a while there was a clunk
as the landing gear came down, and Alix let her
breath out slowly.

'Please remain in your seats, with your seat-belts
fastened, until the aircraft has come to a complete
standstill.' The voice was calm but, to Alix at any
rate, it was a bad landing. The engines seemed to
whine unnervingly and then the wheels bumped and
squeaked, the plane shook and shuddered until all
was quiet.

'It's because of the short runway...' some smart-
alick was saying.

As the door opened, the warm air flooded in.
Alix found her way to the baggage claim area and
grabbed her luggage from the rotary pick-up, which

was not a difficult feat, since only three people had left the plane.

She was on her way to the entrance, and the thick darkness beyond, in search of a taxi when a voice said, 'Miss Sandton?'

She turned. There was an executive chic about her.

'Yes?' Her eyes travelled briefly over the man who had spoken. He could, she thought, be classed as the handsome hunk of the month and although he was obviously prematurely grey, grey was hardly the word to describe his fabulous silver hair. Into the bargain, he was tall and handsome.

'I am Armand Leclerc,' he said.

'Oh, *monsieur*, how *wonderful*!' Alix exclaimed thankfully.

There was a glint of humour in his eyes as he took her bags from her, found a trolley and began pushing it.

'You should have taken a trolley,' he told her.

'I was in too much of a hurry,' she answered, laughing a little. 'Besides, there are just the two of them.' Her eyes went to her cases.

'It's very kind of you to have met me,' she was saying a moment later, as she watched him putting her luggage into his car. 'The plane was madly late. We had electrical problems, as you probably found out for yourself.'

When they were in the car he said, 'We drive now for forty-five minutes, so do not be alarmed, young lady, that I am about to kidnap you.'

'I won't,' she laughed, liking him. It was hard to believe that Camille Boyer was his cousin.

'This is the first time you have visited the island?' He drove competently, but very fast. Alex was aware of the darkness on one side of the car which was due to an enormous mountain. The sea, on the other side, glittered and gathered light from the stars and occasional lights.

'Yes, it is,' she answered. 'I have an appreciation of islands, actually, and always hoped to add La Réunion to my short list.'

'I am sure you will not be disappointed. I hope also that you will enjoy the chalet which I have reserved for you.'

'I'm looking forward to it. Tell me, has the car arrived? I was told it would be delivered to the chalet before I arrived.'

'The car arrived this morning. It is very bright, very yellow, and I hope you will not be shocked. And so I am very interested—you met Reed and my wilful young cousin Camille in Botswana. You were, in fact, their safari guide. If all had gone well for me, I would have been one of your passengers.'

'Maybe next time, although at the moment I'm having a break from safaris,' Alix replied, just to join in.

'And of course you had also on your safari Jacques and Jacquetta and Hugo and Mercedes. You will meet them soon.'

'Oh, how lovely!' She had not banked on this. 'How are they all?'

'Very well. Both young women are awaiting babies. Both are radiant. I conversed with Reed on the telephone recently.'

'So you speak on the phone, now and then?'

'Mostly, on business. Often, though, for pleasure. After all, La Réunion is linked to the rest of the world by satellite and by the direct dialling telephone to France, even if it is very dark at night, for that is what you are thinking, *non*?' Armand's laugh was boyish and charming.

Alix joined in politely, then she said, 'By the way, what's happened about the crocodile farm you planned as a tourist attraction—near your chalets?'

'But of course you know about this. Well, I regret to say the entire concept has collapsed about my ears. The local residents have been gnashing their teeth, so there will be no crocodile farm.'

After a moment Alix said quite honestly, 'I can't say I'm sorry, Monsieur Leclerc. I'm on the side of the islanders, I'm afraid.'

'Ah,' he laughed again, 'do not rub salt on my sore point! We will now change the discussion. By the way, if there is anything you require while you are in the chalet, please do not hesitate to let me know. Everything has been done, I trust, to ensure that your stay here will be a pleasant one. As was explained to you in my letter, the chalet will be serviced and dinner provided, should you be dining at home. It will be cooked by a woman with excellent references. Amongst other recipes she will, I know for sure, prepare for you a medley of recipes from France, from Madagascar and also from India.'

'Oh, wonderful! I'll look forward to them.'

'I think you will enjoy a typical Creole meal—white rice with an accompaniment of curry made with meat or chicken, tossed in oil or butter, maybe, with tomatoes, onions, garlic, saffron, peppers and chillies.'

'I'll eat now and diet later,' laughed Alix.

Although La Réunion was a speck in the ocean, they seemed to have been driving for a long time. Armand was saying, 'You will discover in your chalet an island cocktail awaiting you—to welcome you. It is rather late in the day, unfortunately, since your plane was so late in arriving. You might prefer something else, and you will find in the small kitchen the necessary items to make coffee.'

'Thank you. I think I'm going to go for the cocktail, though,' smiled Alix.

The chalet came as a pleasant surprise. It was furnished mainly with wicker and rattan furniture, and the natural straw materials contributed to the casual style of an island retreat. In the lounge there were also two oversized sofas, upholstered in pink and navy blue striped cotton canvas. A pink orchid, growing in a blue and white Chinese bowl, immediately claimed Alix's attention. There was a separate dining-room, where more rattan furniture prevailed. A break-front housed inexpensive—so Armand told her—Portuguese ware, chosen for its blue and white effect. A chandelier had been created from a blue and white ginger jar and tiny saucers. A plant, with huge exotic broad leaves, stood in a wicker basket.

'You're very trusting,' Alix said, when the inspection was over. 'Sometimes holiday people can be so uncaring—sad, but true. The chalet is absolutely beautiful.'

'This is a special chalet for special people.' Armand smiled at her.

'And so I'm special?' She sounded amused.

'Very special, yes. You are a friend of Reed's and of Camille, my little cousin.'

That's what you think! Alix bit her lip and the fingertips of one hand went beneath her hair, as she touched her neck. She took an unsettled little breath.

'I notice the cyclone shutters at the windows and doors,' she said. 'They look attractive, but even I know that they're in case of cyclones. Let's hope there won't be one while I'm here—or that the volcano doesn't decide to erupt.'

'You are perfectly safe, do not worry. The volcano is on the other side.'

'But it erupted fairly recently, did it not?' she asked.

'That is so. Talking about the volcano, it is not difficult of access. Your car may be driven if wished, on the road leading to the Piton de la Fournaise. Up to the halfway mark the road is tarred. There is a car park there and an excellent view. You do not need to go any further. It is not so good to go up there alone, as you can imagine. Perhaps I can arrange something for you—or drive you myself. Maybe with Reed—who knows? And now, Alix—I am permitted to call you Alix, I hope?'

'Of course.'

'And now I will leave you. Please enjoy your cocktail, and as we say here *à votre santé*, which means your good health.'

After Armand had gone, Alix stood looking around. The roar of the ocean as it pounded the reef—for the chalet was situated on a part of the island which was protected by a reef—seemed to fill the chalet.

She lost no time in running a bath, then slipped into cool satin pyjamas and went out to the balcony. She sat on a peacock chair and sipped her cocktail, which she had found in a small bar refrigerator and where, she noticed, Armand had left a few bottles of this and that. She realised how tired she was, and sleep, in the four-poster bed of giant bamboo, was going to be welcome.

She was awakened by a bird the following morning, as it perched on a cane table next to the sliding doors and pecked on the glass. It was obvious that visitors to the chalets were in the habit of feeding the bird crumbs and directly new tenants moved in it made its presence known to them by tapping.

Armand had explained that it was Alix's responsibility to provide her own breakfasts and lunches, but for this her first morning on the island, a Continental breakfast had been prepared for her. She intended visiting the small shop he had pointed out to her on arrival, after she had eaten and sorted herself out.

From the balcony which ran the full length of the chalet she was able to see the car which was hers during her stay on the island and which, at her request, had been delivered to the chalet. It was a glorious day, and she sat on one of the peacock wicker chairs and bit into the most beautifully coral-hued mango she had ever seen. The golden flesh dripped with juice, and, feeling very contented and rested, she gazed past red, white, pink and deep yellow hibiscus blooms that trembled in the breeze. The waves on the coral reef were sending up sprays of white.

The Creole lady, who had introduced herself as Tharika, and who had prepared Alix's breakfast earlier, came back to clean the chalet, but because of a language barrier, it was impossible to have a conversation. Alix went back inside and changed into white cotton trousers and an olive and candy-pink striped shirt. She had made up her mind to walk to the shop, which stood in a clearing of filao trees. The building was long and low-ceilinged with an almost alarming sloping floor. Parts of the shop were festooned with baskets, and brightly coloured rolls of material filled the shelves. Before making her way to the supermarket section to choose some-thing suitable for breakfasts and lunches, she bought a length of crimson cotton with the words La Réunion printed on it, which she intended to use as a sarong.

Going back to the chalet, she unpacked what she had bought and then decided to try out the car. Maybe if she found a bank, she thought, she would change another travellers' cheque.

As she made her way past a clump of palms to where the car was parked in a carport, she saw Armand walking along the coral-littered beach. His astonishing silver hair blew about in the breeze and he swept it back from his eyes with long tanned fingers. Coming towards her, he called out cheerfully, 'Where are you off to?'

She had a map of the island in her hand. 'I'm going to try out the car, maybe find a bank. It looks simple enough, on the map.'

'How did you sleep?' he asked.

'I slept like a baby. I just passed out.'

He laughed at that. 'But babies do not sleep. They howl most of the night, from what I am given to understand. Why else do you think I have remained a comfortable bachelor?'

Alix smiled at him. 'So you're a bachelor? I wondered. How did you manage to escape?'

'I was clever, Alix.'

'Anyway, Armand, I slept. I've also been to the little shop. I've stocked my refrigerator and my food cupboard.'

There was a pause and then he said, 'By the way, good news—Reed is arriving the day after tomorrow.'

Her heart seemed to take a convulsive leap and his remark left her feeling almost disorientated for a moment, then she recovered.

'Well, well, that must be a surprise for you, Armand. Is he coming to spend a holiday?'

'It is to be a business visit,' Armand replied, 'but he usually combines business with pleasure.'

Alix was longing to ask whether Theresa was coming, but she kept quiet.

Instead she said, 'Well, I must be off. I'll see you later.'

'I hope you will not be too lonely,' he said.

'I came here to *be* lonely, actually. All that concerns me is to do nothing, just relax. I will, of course, drive right round the island one day.' She glanced back at the map. 'I see you can do that. Mmm, perfect!'

Reed was coming. The thought provided little comfort, especially since Armand had explained that it was to be a business visit.

Alix parked the yellow Mini in a small parking area in front of the bank at St Gilles, then after attending to her currency matters she walked right up the winding, busy main street. A strange calm had come over her. No matter what the outcome was going to be, she was going to see Reed again.

The traffic moved incessantly up and down the street. The tarmac shimmered and melted in the sun, and at this moment, it was difficult to believe that she was on a beautiful island in the Indian Ocean.

As she continued to explore the small shops, she noticed that men contemplated her long legs and then her auburn hair, and because she was on her own, she felt embarrassed and hurriedly made her way back to where she had left the Mini.

When she got back to the chalet she changed into a cobalt blue bikini and made her way to the beach, where she stretched out on the sand and closed her eyes. All her thoughts revolved around Reed, and then, feeling a nagging sense of depression, mingled with a certain tense excitement, she got up and went into the water which, protected by the reef, was as calm as a lake. Careful not to hurt her feet on the coral, Alix waded out and began to swim. The world of advertising, game-viewing safaris and even Reed Forsythe seemed very far away at this particular moment.

On the day Reed was to arrive, Armand surprised her by coming to the chalet to enquire whether she would care to drive to the airport with him, and she was immediately plunged into a state of panic as the realisation that she was to come face to face with Reed in the very near future hit her like some wild force.

'I had decided to go and look at a private orchid collection,' she told Armand. 'That's if I can find the place!'

Even while she was speaking, her mind was racing with what she would wear—what she would say...

'I see.' Armand shrugged his shoulders. 'Well, join us for a cocktail at sunset, Alix, at my chalet.'

'That's very kind of you,' she hedged, 'but no. Reed might be jet-lagged, for one thing.'

'I have never known Reed to be jet-lagged.' There was mockery in Armand's eyes. 'Do not press your luck, Alix. I will be over to escort you.'

She made a point of prolonging her day by going to lunch at a little place she had discovered for herself, then leaving so that she would arrive back at her chalet as late in the afternoon as possible.

As she bathed she gazed moodily at the coppery body which had known Reed's lovemaking. Paying her off, he had walked out on her and gone back to Theresa, his wife, which had been on the cards all the time.

Did she want to be caught up in *that* again?

CHAPTER EIGHT

ALIX lifted her shoulder-length hair on top of her head and looked in the mirror as she tried to decide what to wear to Armand's for cocktails. She tried not to think about Reed being there.

Eventually she took out the white cotton pants designed by Jasper and a white singlet top. When she was dressed, she slipped her feet into gold and white sandals and began to comb her auburn hair back from her face. She twisted it into a loose chignon, and found herself wondering what Reed would think of her hair now that it was so much longer. With her tan and glowing health, she knew she did not need make-up, but she expertly touched up her eyes. She was just adjusting her hooped gold earrings when she heard Armand tapping on the glass doors to the lounge, which were open to the sea breezes.

'Coming, Armand!' she called out, and immediately began to shake. 'I won't be a minute.'

He was in the lounge, admiring an arrangement of pink lilies and blue daisies which she had bought at a flower stall.

'Are you looking at the strange combination?' she laughed. 'But they look pretty, don't they? I love pink and blue mixed together, and as it happens, the flowers match the sofas and chairs.'

'I am intrigued by the pink lilies,' he answered, turning to look at her. 'I am of the opinion that someone has used enormous influence in cultivating them. I have not seen pink lilies before, Alix. What are they?'

'They're arums,' she told him.

'But I always understood arums were white?' He looked so serious, she thought, feeling a little amused.

'With cross-pollination anything can happen, Armand. There are also yellow arums, and black. Haven't you seen them?'

'No. Anyway, the result is theatrical, as it was no doubt intended to be. Well, Alix, Reed is here and, emphatically, he is anything but jet-lagged. Shall we go?'

Although Alix appeared charmingly at ease, panic signals were beginning to make their presence known, and right now she would have done anything to put Armand off.

'What about your jacket?' he asked.

She picked up the emerald green and purple silk jacket which she had dropped on the sofa and her thoughts went to the day she had bought it—something really exotic, for the island, was what she'd had in mind.

As they walked to Armand's chalet he said, 'You had, I trust, a pleasant day?'

'Yes, very pleasant.' Her voice was deceptively light. 'Is Reed alone, by the way, Armand?'

'To answer your question—Reed always comes alone. And the orchids? You managed to find the collection?'

'Yes, I did, and I was quite stunned by their beauty. I'll go back again, you can be sure.'

They were still talking when they entered his lounge, and as Alix's eyes went to Reed, any thoughts which she'd harboured that she was over him were immediately dispelled.

He sat, totally at ease, for a moment, then he stood up. Alix had almost forgotten how good-looking he was. He was wearing an impeccably cut lightweight suit. As usual, he wore his hair a little long, and it touched the back of his collar, but he had shaved off his beard and moustache.

'How are you, Alix? So you have decided to visit the island of La Réunion?' His voice was polite—uninterested, almost.

'I always intended to spend a holiday here, and feeling very self-indulgent one day, I reserved a seat on the plane, and here I am.'

'Did you have a good flight?' His eyes held hers, but only briefly, before they went to her mouth.

'Oh, very good.' She decided to be flippant. Reed Forsythe might have hurt her, she was thinking, but she was damned if she was going to show it. 'There were moments, though, when I thought I'd have to place the life-vest over my head, bring the straps to the front and fasten them securely.'

Only Armand laughed. 'Fortunately flying is very safe these days. Sit down, Alix.'

As she moved, she was acutely aware of her perfume which seemed to float about the room, and she wondered whether, in her tense state, while dressing, she had been too liberal with her Giorgio Beverly Hills.

'Thank you, Armand.' She made sure her smile was wide and as beautiful as she knew how, and then, with the utmost grace, she permitted him to take her emerald green and purple silk jacket. Her eyes followed him as he draped it over the arm of a white cotton sofa which looked stunning with raw silk cushions in various shades of island-geranium pink, crimson, honey and green. When she sat down, however, it was not on the sofa but on one of the matching chairs, where she would be sure to remain on her own.

Accepting a cocktail from Armand, she immediately took a sip. 'Mmm, perfect! It's exquisitely cold and delicious. You make the most divine cocktails, Armand. À votre santé.' She lifted long lashes to look at him.

'I intended to bring more ice and I have forgotten the samosas. One moment, please.' Armand went towards the dining-room area and then disappeared from sight into the adjoining kitchen.

Reed's dark blue eyes when he looked across at Alix were as brooding as the Indian Ocean before a severe tropical storm.

'You are, I understand—or was led to understand—no longer with Look-Out Safaris?' In contrast to the expression in his eyes, he spoke lazily.

'It was time for a change. I went back to advertising.' Alix lifted one elegant, slim shoulder, just as lazily. 'So, instead of driving a Land Rover over rough tracks and wearing khaki suits, I now dress elegantly and sit behind a streamlined desk.'

He went on looking at her. 'So you're way up front, as they say?'

'If you mean that as a compliment, thank you. In any case, way up, as they say.' Alix took another sip of her cocktail and noticed that her hand was shaking slightly. I should never have come, she thought.

'And where does all this take place? Gaberone?' he asked.

'Uh-huh.' Deliberately vague, she lifted the glass to her lips.

'Have you sold the cottage and moved into a penthouse, to suit your new life-style?' She saw the challenge in his eyes and assumed a blank expression.

'No, I haven't.' She glanced down at her glass and began moving it about so that the liquid in it began to swirl while her fingers, slim, tanned and beautifully tipped by rose-tinted nails, almost gripped the stem. She was remembering how Reed had callously left money for her, and it was like looking down into a chasm, where the churned-up sea appeared almost tortured. She felt a huge onslaught of humiliation and, looking up, she said, 'I had no idea I'd bump into *you* here.'

He smiled faintly. 'But maybe that's what you hoped for?'

Flooding with anger at his remark, she said quickly, 'Don't kid yourself. I've survived without you, believe me.'

She watched him as he shifted his position and settled back into the cushions. 'Oh, I believe you,' he drawled.

Armand came back with more ice and a platter of samosas. 'More ice for your Scotch, Reed.' He sat down. 'Please help yourselves to samosas when you're ready, Alix. You know, I was very disappointed that I was unable at the very last moment to go on the safari in question. The others—I refer to Jacques, Jacquetta, Hugo and Mercedes—came back with many exiting stories to relate, not to mention copious notes on crocodiles.'

'Your little pipe-dream in other words?' Reed sounded frankly amused.

For a while Alix was able to sit back while a conversation took place, mainly between Armand and Reed. Her eyes condemned Reed, as she brooded and sipped her cocktail.

'These wild game-viewing safaris must create much excitement,' Armand tried to draw her back into the conversation.

Her gaze was almost catlike. 'You'd better ask Reed about that.'

Reed's soft laugh was suggestive. 'Now that really would be telling, wouldn't it?'

'In any case, Armand, when it comes to a game-viewing safari—or rather, when it *came* to a game-viewing safari, since I've now left Look-Out Safaris—I merely did my job. For me, no matter what happened, how much excitement, it was always a case of one more safari. Reed demanded good service, by the way.' There was a hard edge to her voice. 'And he got it.'

Reed raised his glass. 'And, Alix, I was not disappointed. I think you're aware of that.' He spoke with a deliberate, brutal kind of carelessness.

After a few moments Alix stood up and reached for her silk jacket. 'Thank you, Armand, that was nice. I really must go now, if you don't mind.'

'But why, Alix?' He was already on his feet.

'Well, I've had quite a day. I drove to see the orchid collection, as you know, and I went to lunch...I'll come another time and I'll stay longer—that's a promise.'

'Since I feel like a breath of sea air after my long flight, I'll see Alix back to her chalet,' said Reed, a bit too casually.

For Armand's sake Alix kept quiet, but when they were outside she said, 'Reed, appearing polite in front of Armand is one thing, but employing contrivance to get me alone is quite another. I don't need an escort. Your turning up here is a disaster, let me tell you that.'

He laughed at that. 'Perhaps, my dear girl, I should remind you that I often come to this little French island in the Indian Ocean, whereas you, on the other hand, do not. Nevertheless, you mentioned that you'd survived without me and I should imagine the same will happen here. You will go on surviving—and so will I.'

'While we're having this intimate little tête-à-tête, Mr Forsythe, I don't ever want to discuss the safari or to be reminded of it. After all, what happened between us in the Chobe Game Reserve really amounted to very little.'

'Maybe, but it was fantastic while it lasted, right?' Reed sounded furious, and Alix caught her breath as he stopped walking to take her roughly by the shoulders. She could just make out his face in the darkness.

'There was nothing fantastic about it. As far as I was concerned, I suddenly decided that now was a good time—and what better way than to have that happen on safari with a handsome, bearded tourist?'

'And so you found me obliging? I've often wondered what was wrong with the fair, fragile and handsome Gerald?'

'Leave Gerald out of this! What it amounted to is—you helped me and I helped you.' There must be a limit to this madness, Alix was thinking. She moved away from him.

'What exactly makes you think you helped me, Alix? What did you think I was? Some sort of sex-deprived, stunted village oaf?'

'Look, having gone into my first affair with *mature deliberation*, I don't want to be reminded of it,' she snapped. 'It suited me to become your substitute bedmate for a couple of hours, and it meant as much to me as it meant to you. *You* were using me. *I* was using you.'

'And how were affairs number two, and three and four?' he asked coldly.

He made no attempt to follow her when she left him and started to run towards her chalet, but she knew he was still there, watching her.

While the chalet basked in the morning sun, Alix slept on the next morning. She had been awake for half the night and only the persistent knocking of Tharika finally dragged her from the heavy sleep of exhaustion.

As she ate her breakfast—grapefruit segments with avocado—on the balcony, she brooded on Reed and the way in which she had brought him back into her life, just by coming to the island. She had only herself to blame for what was happening now. Against her better judgement, she had come to La Réunion when she knew the possibility existed that she would cross paths with Reed; or she *could*. The possibility might have been slight, but it *had* existed. She'd known from the start that Reed had business interests on the island.

When Armand had told her that Reed was arriving she had experienced an electric shock of promise, until she had made the shattering discovery that he was merely on another business visit and that his visit was purely coincidental and had absolutely nothing to do with her.

She felt restless and lonely, the island had suddenly lost its appeal, and the thought of spending a holiday on it was causing her to have second thoughts. Fortunately, she thought, she had hired a car, and she would make sure she used it. She reached for the map which she had brought out to the balcony and which she had put on the cane table.

She was studying it when Reed came up the steps at the far end, and she saw his blue eyes going over her white shorts and apricot-coloured shirt.

'So, Alix, you're still chasing the sun? Maybe tomorrow's sun will be even better. Who knows?'

'Is that all you've come to say?'

'No. You've grown your wonderful hair, I see.'

She felt manipulated. 'Look, I'm busy right now.'

'Don't be sarcastic, Alix. I'm just not in the mood for it. You look anything but busy to me. Since we're practically neighbours I suggest we make the best of it.'

'Of a bad job, you mean?'

'I didn't say that—you did. Right? Look, I'm going to visit the stud farm in a few minutes. Come with me.' His voice sounded almost friendly.

'Why?' she asked. There was hostility in hers.

'Apart from your gaining an insight into what goes on in a useless playboy's life, the drive is very scenic. Why drive yourself about when I can do that for you?'

After a moment she said, 'I had intended to drive to see a Tamil temple.'

'You'll see a Tamil temple on the way.'

'I told you last night...'

'Forget about what you told me last night,' Reed interrupted. 'There are no risks. You referred to your "mature deliberation", however. I'm sure that same mature deliberation will see you all right this time.'

'OK, I'll come, and I'll kick myself later. When exactly are you leaving?'

He glanced at his watch—the Concord which he had worn in Botswana and which had reminded Alix of Theresa, for some unknown reason.

'Let's say in about twenty minutes?' Reed lifted his lashes. 'Will that suit you?'

'That will be fine. I'd like to change,' she told him.

'Afterwards I'll take you to lunch.' He looked at her in a way that made her pulse race. 'Come along to Armand's chalet when you're ready. I'll meet you there.'

After he had left her, she went into her bedroom and looked out a plain white shift and her white and gold sandals and changed into them. She combed her hair back from her face and arranged it in a loose chignon, applied lip-gloss, then checked herself in the mirror. Earrings? The large round ones made of honey-gold metal, to match her eyes.

Reed was waiting for her on the lawn of Armand's chalet, and she was engulfed in pleasure just by seeing him there. He was wearing white canvas pants, and she wondered whether they were the same ones he had worn in the game reserve. His deep purple islandish shirt did wonderful things to his dark blue eyes.

She glanced around, her eyes searching for Armand, and sensing this, Reed said, 'Armand has gone out.'

'So Armand isn't coming?' Alix turned to look at him.

'Did you think he was coming?'

'Well, yes, as a matter of fact I did think so.'

'Does it make any difference?' There was a touch of anger in his voice.

'No, it doesn't make any difference.' She masked her feelings by giving him a cool stare.

'OK, Alix, let's go. I'll show you what my life is all about. It's not all a case of wine, women and song, believe me ... if you can bring yourself to do that.'

As he had remarked, the drive to the stud farm was nothing short of spectacular, and it was easy to see why the island was described as 'emerging from the Indian Ocean as a huge dome of basalt'. While the area of the volcano might be nothing but desolate craters, the interior was beautiful, with forests, jagged gorges and mountain peaks, wreathed in mist. Lava formations contrasted with lush, and in the flat areas there were many geranium fields and lots of swaying sugar cane. They were on a road high above the lava coastline which, without the offshore protection of an encircling reef, faced the full savage onslaught of the Indian Ocean.

Reed pointed out things which he thought might interest Alix; a colourful market-place, as they passed through a small town, a waterfall tucked high between two mountains—he stopped the car here, and moved right over to her and put his arm about her shoulder so that he could get her to focus her gaze in the right direction—a candle burning gold in a shrine, a forest of pandanus. He kept his promise about the Tamil temple. During the entire drive Alix remembered how it had been as she had lain spent in his arms after their lovemaking. From time to time, her moody eyes rested on his tanned hands and then she would turn away to stare at those mysterious, cloud-draped silhouettes of the mountain tops, wondering what the outcome of meeting up with Reed was going to be.

He surprised her by asking, 'Are you with Gerald?'

'I don't think I need to answer that.' She had to fight her frustrated anger.

'I should have thought your relationship would have thrived after you'd decided to take the—er—mature plunge with me.' His face had a hard and unyielding look about it now.

The anger in her was coming out. 'What's it to you, anyway?' she demanded.

'I won't pretend I'm not interested, Alix.'

'Well, I have no intention of discussing my sex life with you. That must be upsetting for you, mustn't it?'

'Oh, not half as upsetting as when you had all my letters returned to me by Look-Out Safaris.' Reed did not sound very upset, Alix thought bitterly. After a moment he went on, 'I found you very exciting then, Alix. I still do, make no mistake.'

'Well, I am, after all, capable of great excitement,' she answered in a brittle voice. 'Anyway, what's the big deal? It was just a—let's say—a collision of passions, wasn't it?'

He laughed at that. 'Ha, and you have no doubt enjoyed more passions since then. After all, the sole reason was that you wanted to be liberated, and what better way than by a handsome—your description, not mine—bearded tourist. I paved the way for your future escapades, it would appear.'

They had reached tall white gates which were open to green lawns, low white wooden fences and stables. A track of tan ran round the huge centre lawn and a number of horses were in the process of being exercised.

Reed continued along the long avenue, flanked by more low wooden fences and trees, then he parked the car in front of a large white two-storied house with a red-painted roof. The house was extremely well kept but obviously very old, and it reminded Alix of a plantation house, with its downstairs and upper verandas, which ran the entire length of the house.

A few moments later she was being introduced to the compound manager and his wife and tea was served on the downstairs veranda. Finally Reed said, 'This will indicate, to a lesser extent, of course, what my life in Chantilly is all about, Alix. Are you ready to be shown round?' His eyes held hers.

'Yes.' Alix turned to the wife of the compound manager. 'Thank you for the tea and the sweet potato pie.'

The stables were impeccable. Horses gazed out from the stalls, which were shaded by a long brick veranda. Other horses were tied outside, waiting to be groomed. Alix noticed the head-collars, each bearing the exotic names of the horses, which were hung beside each stall—names like Sherri, Yasmin, Wild Jewel, Flame Lily, Desert Star and Sega.

Reed explained what the woven grass roll-up blinds were for. 'They're let down when the sun slants into the stalls and they're then sprinkled with water to promote coolness.' He took Alix by the arm, as he guided her past a hosepipe, which had been left lying across the brick floor. 'Careful!'

She felt a thrill as his fingers touched her skin.

As she thrilled to his touch she murmured, 'I'm very impressed. It's very five-star, isn't it?'

For her benefit, a groom fed the horses sugar-lumps, which he kept in his pocket, then he passed her one.

'You make friends with Maloya,' he ordered.

As Alix took the sugar she asked, 'What does Maloya mean?' She glanced at Reed.

'Smart Alix!' he laughed softly.

'But not smart enough, right?' She felt her gaze flickering.

'I'd say you were very smart,' answered Reed, 'but, to get back to what Maloya means. Here in La Réunion we have the dance of the sega, as you probably know. Maloya was, at the beginning, a dance of the slaves. After a day's work, the slaves would gather together to sing songs, telling of their pain. The rhythm of the music was slow and hyp-notic—and nothing like this horse, by the way.'

Alix held out the sugar and the horse strained its neck, laid back its ears and showed the whites of its eyes, and she got such a fright that she stepped back hastily and would have fallen if Reed, who was standing slightly behind her, had not put his arms around her. He held her close against him and she felt his hard thighs against the backs of her legs, and for a moment she felt herself drowning in his embrace. 'This reminds me of a girl wearing leg-warmers and not much else,' she heard him say against the nape of her neck. 'Remember the Grewia Lodge and the ice-cold water from the de-frosting refrigerator—or don't you permit yourself to do that?'

As she broke away from him she said to the amused groom, 'I'm sorry, I—I've dropped the sugar. I thought the horse was going to bite me,' then she listened to Reed as he explained, in French, that Miss Sandton was a wild-game safari guide in a vast game reserve, and although she was in the habit of coping with elephants, lions and other dangerous animals, she was, apparently, afraid of horses. This was translated to her later, and the story had greatly amused the Creole groom and she found herself laughing with him.

After a few moments, Alix took an unsettled little breath. 'Reed, I'm curious to know what prompted you to breed and train racehorses. Was it—er—just your love of horses?'

'Blame my great-grandfather.' His tone was mocking. 'He must have passed the bug on to me.'

'Do you always have to blame someone?'

'Well, if *I* don't, *you* will.' His eyes held hers. 'In any case, when my great-grandfather retired from the Army in India, he began breeding and training horses and, as I've said, he must have passed the bug on to me.'

At the end of the tour he said, 'And now I'm taking you to lunch. I hope you're hungry. Are you?'

'Well, yes, I am, actually.'

They laughed, holding eyes. 'So am I,' said Reed. 'It's lonely where we're going, by the way. People go there for the good food and the excellent views. Tourists are told about it and they often hire a taxi for the day, or do a mini-coach excursion. That's how it keeps going. It's a place in which to enjoy lunch only. The restaurant doesn't serve dinners. I think we should talk there.'

'Talk? What about, Reed? Theresa?'

'Why do you drag Theresa into this?' His voice was almost harsh.

'Why, indeed?' answered Alix, and the remark was followed by an angry silence.

The place was Cap Méchant on the southern coastal region, and, set amidst a profusion of pandanus palms, wind-bent trees, ferns and ginger plants in flower, it was, as he had explained, lonely. From the area in which he had parked the car, they could look down at the sea which blasted the black lava rocks far below, sending up high cascades of white water as it was dashed against the black-cliffed coastline. Looking inland, there were views of the masses of lava trails down the distant mountain slopes, which were also thick with forest. There was a smell of mist and damp.

Apart from two middle-aged men who were involved in conversation, they were the only guests. They sat at a pink-clothed table, and there was, thought Alix, a sense of unreality about being with the man she loved again.

The chef arrived at their table and went to some length to explain the meal they were about to enjoy; fish cooked in ginger and delicious poulet Coco stemmed from the Comoro Islands. A salad of palm hearts, a dish special to La Réunion, would be placed to one side, for sampling.

While she listened, Alix stared down at the ring which her mother had given her; one large lustrous pink-sheened pearl, set on a pile of gold. She had noticed Reed's eyes going to it, soon after she had settled herself amongst the cushions in Armand's large comfortable chair the night before.

When they were alone again he said, 'So you've become a successful business woman and see life from behind a huge, uncluttered desk.'

'I didn't say it was uncluttered. I said it was streamlined. Actually, at times it's *very* cluttered.' Her eyes accused him. 'I'm trying not to take offence here.'

'Cluttered—what with?' Reed's tone was still slightly mocking.

'Cluttered with such things as reports, letters, folders, proofs, photo-sheets, visuals, telephones...do you want me to go on?'

He laughed softly and she went on. 'You sound surprised. Don't you think I'm capable enough to be sitting behind a desk?'

'Oh, come, Alix!'

'By the way, I forgot to mention the specimen vase,' Alix added. 'My smooth-voiced secretary *always* sees to it that there is always one perfect orchid in it.' Her voice contained sarcasm.

'So?' He went on regarding her. 'I hope you don't spoil all this by wearing large horn-rimmed glasses. Do you?' She saw the groove in one cheek deepening.

'No, I don't.' She refused to be ruffled. 'My glasses are fashionable, with large frames. I find your mockery amusing, Reed.'

'Indeed? Tell me, did you find it amusing when you had my letters returned to me by your friend Karl Sievewright from Look-Out Safaris?' His deep blue eyes were brilliant against the tan of his skin.

'Reed, it beats me why we should be sitting here raking up the past in which you treated me as a sex object and then, when things were getting too hot for you, you hopped into some executive jet and took off. How convenient, for you that there just happened to be a conference at the Sycamore Safari Lodge! I'm beginning to ask myself just what the hell I'm doing here with you.' Her fingers sought the comfort of the pink pearl again.

'Perhaps it might interest you, Alix, to hear that I looked everywhere for you at the lodge before I hopped into that executive jet and took off—and yes, how convenient for me that there just hap-

pened to be a conference at the safari lodge just
when I needed an airlift so desperately. Where were
you, by the way?'

'Why do we keep talking about that? It's over.
I've given up losing sleep over you ages ago.' Alix
stopped talking as their food arrived and they ate
in silence for a while.

'We'll talk later,' said Reed, breaking the silence.

'What about?' She lifted her lashes to look at
him.

'About us. What else?' His response was one of
fury.

'There's nothing to talk about, and you know it.'

After lunch was over, they went out to the car,
which was parked next to one other car, then Alix
went to stand at the heavy black wooden railing
fence and gazed down at the huge cascades of white
spray where the ocean battered the black cliffs of
the shoreline.

Suddenly she felt near to tears and reached into
her bag for her sunglasses—then she realised that
she had left them on the lunch table.

'I've forgotten my sunglasses. I'll go back for
them...'

'Wait here,' said Reed, 'I'll go and get them.'

'No! I'll do it myself.' She was already running
from him.

She was on her way back to the car again when
she noticed the two men who had lunched at the
restaurant, and it was obvious that they had been
for a short walk and were now on their way back

to their car, which was parked next to the car Reed had hired.

On a wild impulse, Alix went up to them and they looked at her in surprise when she said, 'Excuse me, but do you speak English?'

It turned out that they did—they spread their hands—a little.

'Are you going anywhere near St Gilles?' she asked. 'If so, may I go back with you in your car? You see, I've quarrelled with my friend and I have no wish to go back with him.'

Although they both appeared to be embarrassed by her request, it was agreed that if she so wished she could go back with them.

Going back to Reed, she said, 'Reed, I've decided to go back with those two men over there. It just doesn't make sense, our being together, when there's absolutely no future to it.'

'You're not going back with them. I forbid it, Alix!' snapped Reed.

'And just who are you to forbid me anything? I don't want to be involved with you.'

'You are involved with me, Alix! Get in the car.'

Their eyes clung together in hostility. 'I will not allow you to go back with these men. What the hell do you think I am?' Reed demanded angrily.

'They're respectable, elderly men.'

'And I'm not respectable, is that it?' His deep blue eyes were furious.

'While you've been going on about things, you've completely overlooked the fact that you did a despicable thing before you left the Sycamore Safari Lodge. Just keep away from me in future.'

Alix turned to leave, but he reached out and caught her wrist and swung her round to face him. 'What did I do?'

'What did you *do*?' Her eyes were wide and angry, and she wrenched her wrist away from his tight fingers. 'Think about it! *Just think about it!*'

'Get in the car, Alix.'

'I have no intention of going back with you!' she retorted.

'OK. Do as you bloody well like,' he told her before he went over to his car and got into it and slammed the door.

The first thing Alix did when she got back to her chalet was run a bath, then she lay in the warm geranium-scented water and abandoned herself to sheer misery.

She had just got out of the bath and was wrapped in the folds of a white towelling robe when Reed arrived.

'You have absolutely no sensitivity!' she told him furiously. 'Why have you come here? Haven't I made it clear enough that I don't want to have anything to do with you? Why don't you get back where you belong?'

'You know damn well why I've come, Alix. I've come to try and sort something out. We've lost enough time. I came to La Réunion when I heard that you were renting one of Armand's chalets, because I wanted to hear, first hand, what the hell went wrong.'

'You know what the hell went wrong. Tell me, did you pay them all? Or was it just *me*? I didn't think I was all that good. After all, it was the first time for me. I must have been a disappointment, right?'

'For God's sake, Alix, you know what that money was for!'

'What was it for—as if I don't know?'

'It was a courtesy token to a professional guide.'

'Oh, sure. Don't remind me,' said Alix bitterly. 'I became a professional when I went to bed with you. Why don't you just go back to your wife, where you belong?'

He looked shocked beyond belief. 'You can't be serious, Alix. What the devil are you talking about—*my wife*?'

'Theresa, Reed. Theresa. Remember her? You have a habit of forgetting her when you're with me.'

'Theresa was not my wife, for God's sake!'

'Really?' There was disbelief in Alix's voice. 'Well, that's not what Camille told me...'

'Not what Camille told you? Camille again! She left nothing out, it seems, except *my side* of the story. And you believed her?' Reed caught her to him. 'You believed this immature girl's word against mine?'

'Let go of me!' Alix snapped. She pushed him away and staggered back, clutching at the neckline of her robe. 'She was mature enough for you to have taken her to bed with you, wasn't she?'

'Is that what you believe? And I suppose she told you that as well. I don't have to explain that damned girl to you, Alix. Let's just say she was easily available but left me cold. She invited herself to my tent, and later my chalet, but...'

'And what about all the others?' Alix hardly knew what she was saying now. 'Did you *pay* them?'

'Do you want me to list them?' Reed asked furiously. 'I can assure you, it won't take long. But— Theresa my wife, and you believed it? Whew, Alix, I'm beginning to think I don't understand anything about you! I can't believe it.' He went on staring at her. 'God!' It was said on a long shocked breath. 'And you believed her!'

Trying to adjust to the fact that Reed was not married and feeling almost stunned, Alix said, 'I thought you were married. It seemed feasible. You were a mystery to me at times, and Camille said...'

'You thought! Camille said! I asked you in the letter I wrote before I left the Sycamore Safari Lodge to *trust* me. Maybe you should have given it a try, eh? Trust is, after all, what a relationship is all about.'

In a very soft voice she asked, 'Is there something I don't know? There was no letter. Just the money in an envelope marked Alix. You left it with Camille to give me. Do you remember now? Or are you suffering from loss of memory, Reed?'

He was quiet so long that she thought he was not going to answer her, and then he said, 'There's something very wrong here. Let's get to the bottom of this. You say Camille *gave* you the envelope?'

Alix's heart began to freeze. She took the letter out, she was thinking. She used another envelope and printed my name on it and she left the money for me. 'Yes. She gave me the envelope which contained money.'

'In the first place,' said Reed, 'Camille had nothing to do with this. I wrote a short letter to you and explained what had happened and why I was leaving in such a hurry. I took it along to your chalet and put it on the cane table next to your bed, where you'd see it when you got back from wherever you were.' His voice was bitter. 'Anyway, that's beside the point. You know what's happened, don't you? She went along to your chalet, after I'd gone, and helped herself to the letter.'

Alix went on looking at him in bewilderment, then she sat down.

Reed stared down at her with growing anger. 'But in any case, I wrote later, giving you the full story, when I got back to France. If you'd taken delivery of the letter I addressed care of Look-Out Safaris, Alix, you would have made that discovery for yourself. Instead, my letter was returned to me by Karl Sievewright, along with a note telling me, on your behalf, to get lost. I wrote again, on the offchance that you'd change your mind and collect the letters yourself. God, Alix, how could you have done it?'

Alix was so upset that she began to cry, but Reed made no attempt to comfort her, so after a few minutes, she got up and went to her bedroom for a tissue. Her neck ached with tension. She slipped out of the white towelling robe and got into a deep purple caftan, then, still in her bare feet, she went through to the lounge.

Reed was at the glass doors, staring out, and he turned when he heard her.

'What was in the letter,' she asked, very softly, 'that caused you to leave in such a hurry?'

'Theresa was a friend, who stayed with me for a couple of months. I was sorry for her. She was beautiful and that's about all, actually. She asked me whether I'd put her up for a while, since she'd been asked to leave her apartment. The building, she said, was being torn down to make way for a modern block.' He shrugged.

'You talk—in the past tense,' Alix said in a low frightened voice.

'Theresa is dead.'

'Oh, no!' Alix took a long breath and covered her face with her hands and when she dropped them she said, 'Why? How?'

'I'd better start from the beginning. You'll understand better—I think. She—er—was into drugs, as they say. Believe me, *I* didn't know. I began to notice that she was often depressed. I also discovered that she was shoplifting, and when I challenged her about this, she confessed to feeling alive when she shoplifted. What would you have done? I tried to help her but it was no use. She seemed to have no trouble in finding a place and she left, taking all her belongings. She was seeing another man. It meant nothing to me. Believe it or not, she was the first—and last—woman to live in my château.'

'Do you realise how depressing all this is?' Alix's voice broke. She had to gulp for air.

'Do you want me to go on? It's entirely up to you, Alix.'

'Of course I want you to go on—what else?'

'Apparently, soon after I left for Botswana, Theresa went back to the château and she spun a long tale to my housekeeper, who believed her. She said I'd given her permission to use the château, which was nonsense. Apparently this man went with her, but left soon afterwards, according to my housekeeper. Theresa was found unconscious. She'd taken an overdose and she was rushed to hospital, but she didn't survive. But—and this was what lay behind the terrible urgency to get back to France—a large quantity of drugs were found in my home. In other words, through no fault of mine—but I yet had to prove this—I was in trouble. Drugs, in any country, are bad news. But to get back to when we arrived at the Sycamore Safari Lodge. There was a note pinned on my door, requesting me to go along to Reception. The note was marked urgent. When I got to Reception, I was told that the Holiday Inn in Gaberone had phoned. It's always been my policy to leave an itinerary behind with my secretary, and I also made it clear that while I was in the Chobe Game Reserve the Holiday Inn would handle any urgent phone calls, should there be any from France or England. The Holiday Inn had phoned the Sycamore, and I duly rang back, to be told that my lawyer had phoned from France, saying it was imperative that I should get in touch as soon as possible. As you can imagine, I wondered what the devil was going on at home. Reception put me on to a man who was leaving for Gaberone almost immediately, and the outcome was that he offered me a seat on a four-seater plane. I went back to the chalet to tell you of my plans, but I was damned if I could find you. There was just time to pack and write you a short letter.'

Alix's thoughts rushed to the way-out-of-sight bench which overlooked the river and where she had sat with Werner from Early Bird Safaris, while some rebellious part of her mind was determined to keep Reed waiting for her, just as she had waited for him.

'I wrote to you from France, Alix, explaining everything from beginning to end and asking you once again to have faith in me and trust me. Each time my letters were returned with a note saying that Alix Sandton had issued instructions to the effect that I should get lost.'

'Were your letters opened by Karl?' she asked, feeling sick.

'No, they weren't opened, as it happened. They were merely put in another envelope and sent back. Apart from having my address on the back of the envelopes, Sievewright has it in his books, as you probably know. In all fairness to him, I suppose if he *had* opened them, he would have realised that I wasn't playing games with you.'

After a while Alix said, 'No one likes to hear that about—Theresa.'

When Reed came over to her and tried to take her in his arms she exclaimed, 'No, don't touch me! Don't touch me!'

'You don't trust me, is that it? You still haven't learned to believe in me.'

'I haven't got much cause to.' She pushed the tears upwards from her cheeks.

'I'm damned if I'm going to lose you again, Alix! That is, if you care—do you?'

'You know I do.'

'There have been women in my life,' Reed admitted, 'but I've never *loved* someone—and that's the truth. When I went back to France it was to be no more than *au revoir*, Alix. I was coming back to Botswana for you at the first possible moment, to ask you to marry me. That was before the anger took over. I thought—well, if that's the way it is with Alix, she can go to hell for all I care. I did care, though, and you were in my thoughts constantly. Maybe you're not going to believe this, but I'm hoping you will... I'd already made plans to go to Botswana when Armand phoned to say that you were coming to the island. It was nothing short of mental telepathy.'

Alix did not resist him this time, as he put his arms about her.

'Do you believe in mental telepathy?' Reed's voice was very soft.

She nodded, unable to speak.

'Stop crying, darling. You belong to me, Alix, and I belong to you.'

He kissed her and went on kissing her.

'Say something, Alix! Can you love me again?'

'I do love you. I've missed you. I feel—frantic with—wanting you...'

As he lifted her up and carried her to her bedroom he said, 'That makes two of us—I'm frantic with wanting you...' As he slipped her caftan off her shoulders he said, 'And that's the way it's going to be for a long, long time. Make up your mind for it, my wife-to-be.'

The caftan rustled to the floor.

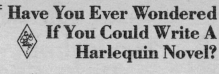

Have You Ever Wondered If You Could Write A Harlequin Novel?

Here's great news—Harlequin is offering a series of cassette tapes to help you do just that. Written by Harlequin editors, these tapes give practical advice on how to make your characters—and your story—come alive. There's a tape for each contemporary romance series Harlequin publishes.

Mail order only

All sales final
